The Calling

To Angela —

Lily Graison

So nice to meet you,

All the best,

Lily Graison

This is a work of fiction. All characters, names, places and incidents in this publication are purely fictitious and are the result of the author's imagination. Any resemblance to actual events, locations, organizations or persons, living or dead, is purely coincidental.

First paperback printing November 2011
First Edition

The Calling
A Night Breeds Novel
© 2010 Lily Graison
ISBN – 1451535481
ISBN – 978-1451535488
www.lilygraison.com

All rights reserved.

No part of this publication may be reproduced, stored in a retrieval system, or transmitted, in any form or by any means mechanical, electronic, photocopying, recording or otherwise without the prior written consent of the publisher, nor be otherwise circulated in any form of binding or cover other than that in which it is published and without a similar condition being imposed on the subsequent purchaser.

Printed in the United States of America

Acknowledgements

To Sid....

For always having an idea when I don't. I'd never get anything done without your input.

One

The stench from the alley caused Rayna's stomach to heave. Rotting flesh, the coppery tang of blood, and the scent of human waste triggered her gag reflex. Holding her breath helped ward off some of the smell but the images of the girl would follow her into nightmares for weeks to come.

The blaring wail of rescue vehicles grew louder. Steeling her nerves to see everything she could before she was forced to leave, she took a step closer to the body to get a better look.

"You do realize you're standing in a puddle of blood, right?"

Rayna jumped, startled by the voice, and glanced down, hissing a curse at the thick, black sludge under her feet before taking a step back. She frowned at the dark splotches that were now smeared on the edge of her sneakers. Something thick and meaty was stuck to the toe of her shoe and she scraped her foot across the ground, dislodging the chunk of lord knows what that was hanging there, and felt her stomach turn again.

"Why are you at my crime scene, Ms. Ford? You're trampling on my evidence."

She knew without looking who was behind her. The condescending tone of voice told her it was Garrett.

The Calling

Turning her head to look over her shoulder confirmed it. He didn't look happy either.

Of course, it may have been the fact that he looked as if he'd just crawled out of bed. His white button-up shirt had more wrinkles than a Shar Pei pup, his tie was crooked and the suit jacket he wore was just as wrinkled as his shirt. His black trousers weren't much better. He also suffered from one serious case of bed-head. His dark locks were tousled and thrown askew. A days worth of stubble marred his handsome face and she cringed when she saw fire in his tawny brown eyes.

She straightened her shoulders and turned to face him. "The same reason you are," she said, using the same clipped tones he'd used with her. "To find out who's behind the series of murders plaguing our fair city."

"Bullshit," Garrett laughed. "You're after your story. You could care less who or what it is as long as your name gets put on the front page of the newspaper."

"That's harsh, Garrett."

"It's also the truth." He crossed his arms over his chest, which made his shoulders look impossibly wide, and studied her for long minutes before a tiny smile lifted the corner of his mouth. "Tell me, Rayna, I'm curious, are all reporters vultures or is that just something you've mastered?"

Rayna felt the jab like a fist to the gut. She stared at him, seeing the contempt in his eyes and wondered why he hated her so much. Just because their little affair went sour wasn't a reason for him to go out of his way to offend her every time she saw him. He was the one who decided it was over, not her, but that didn't stop his prickly jabs every time she crossed his path, which meant she was getting insulted on a weekly basis.

She studied his face, wondering how they ever managed to carry on a half decent conversation. He was still the same egotistical asshole he always had been. Smug, cocky, irritating. And way too damn easy on the eyes. The fact she still enjoyed looking at him only made her ire at him more intense. No matter how big an asshole Garrett Kincaid was, her treacherous pulse raced just a little bit faster every time she saw him.

Ignoring his barbed comment, and how said pulse was beginning to race, she smiled and said, "Well, someone has to report what you guys fail to release to the public, Detective Kincaid."

"So making yourself at home during a formal investigation is your way of what? Doing your civic duty? I should have you arrested for crossing the police line."

"You could," she said, "but you won't." She hoped like hell he wouldn't. The last time she'd crossed the police barricade he'd hauled her all the way to the police station before letting her go. Hopefully tonight wouldn't be a repeat of that bit of drama.

"And what makes you so sure I won't?"

She smiled at him and tilted her head to one side. "Because if you arrest me, that means you'll have to spend hours dealing with me and we both know the sight of me infuriates you for some unknown reason."

He heaved a heavy sigh and glanced around the alley before facing her again. "What are you doing here, Rayna?"

"I'm a reporter, Garrett, and another dead body equals news," she said smugly. Digging her voice recorder out of her bag, she turned it on before flashing him a saccharine smile. "Tell me Detective Kincaid, what do the residents of Bluff's Point need to do to keep themselves safe from the Night Stalker?"

"The Night Stalker?" He gave her an appalled look. "Christ, Rayna. Don't go printing that shit in the paper. If you give this creep a name it'll only give him more reason to hunt."

"He's going to do that anyway. How many are dead now, Garrett?"

He stared at her. "Five."

"Exactly. You have a serial killer on your hands, just like my last story indicated. It's my job to tell anyone who will listen what this guy gets off on." He didn't look too pleased with that fact. She ignored his stare and extended her arm, holding the voice recorder out to him and asked, "Was the victim sexually assaulted?"

He ran a hand over his face and looked over his shoulder. The alley was starting to fill with officers, the choppy static of voices coming through walkie-talkies filling the air. He ran a hand through his hair before turning back to face her. "We're not playing this game tonight, Rayna. You've got all the information you're going to get. I'm tired, the chief has been all over my ass for weeks now because of you and your little investigations and you being here isn't going to help my case any. I want you out of here."

"Oh, come on, Garrett," she said, resisting the urge to stomp her foot like a child. "Give me something to go on and I'll leave."

"Go home, Rayna."

She watched him for long moments before turning to look back at the body. Her stomach tried to revolt again at the sight of it. The poor girl had been nearly torn apart. Luckily it was dark enough that the bits and pieces that looked like torn clothing would let her mind think it was, but deep down she knew better.

The girl's chest was ripped open. The stench of blood and other things rolled her stomach and made her dinner sour and threaten to come back up. She'd been holding her breath before Garrett showed up. The verbal sparring with him hadn't afforded her the luxury any longer and she could smell the death that clung to the girl and the rotten waste in the alley.

Resisting the urge to cover her nose with her hand, she sucked in a sharp breath through her mouth and said, "This looks like an animal attack. Is that something new or has the police department been keeping secrets again?" She turned away from the body, putting her back to it, and took a few steps closer to Garrett. "The public has a right to know these things. How many dead women will it take before the real story finally reaches them?"

Rayna knew she crossed the line the moment Garrett's handsome face contorted. His jaw clenched, his eyes narrowing as anger washed over his features. She took a step back when he advanced on her and grabbed her arms.

"You just don't know when to let go, do you? This isn't a game, Rayna. People are dying. Women. Do you want to be next?"

The Calling

"I won't be if you'll tell me what I need to look out for! Why all the secrets, Garrett? What is it the police don't want us to know?"

He stared down at her, their noses almost touching. She could feel his breath on her face; smell the clean, fresh scent of his skin. The heat from his body scorched her flesh where he touched her and she realized too late she'd leaned into him, their bodies now flush. His gaze never faltered, the anger she saw on his face slowly sliding away and he tilted his head just enough to make her think he was going to kiss her. To her disappointment, he didn't.

The anger returned a moment later but the fierce look in his eyes had changed, replaced with something she'd never seen within him before. Fear. He was scared. She could see it as he stared down at her, feel it in the way he held his body and in the small tremble in his voice. But scared of what and why? She swallowed the lump that formed in her throat and tried to ignore how good it felt to have him so close. "Talk to me, Garrett."

His gaze traveled her face, sweeping across her features before landing on her lips. "Go home, Rayna," he said softly, letting go of her and taking a step back. She felt the loss immediately.

"When will the official police report be available?"

"You'll be the first to know." He turned and walked away without another word, leaving her to stand amongst the flashing lights of rescue vehicles and the stagnant smells only a dirty alley could produce.

Rayna studied his retreating form. Since when did Garrett not give her something to go on? He might hate her now since she wasn't sharing his bed but he always threw her some tiny bit of information just to get rid of her. "I guess the honeymoon really is over," she said to herself.

Sighing, she glanced at her watch. She had just enough time to type up her report, sketchy as it was, and get it to the newsroom for the morning edition. She turned the voice recorder off and stuffed it into her bag, looking around the alley one last time before turning and walking to her car. She had all the information she was going to get tonight. For whatever reason, Garrett didn't want to play anymore.

Garrett stood at the end of the alley and watched Rayna's car pull out onto the street. The taillights flashed, painting the night bright red before blinking out. When she rounded the corner and left his line of sight, he turned and walked back to the victim, staring down at her. The blood around the girl's body spread across the pavement in a large black puddle. The sight of it caused his teeth to ache. He could taste it on the back of his tongue, smell its stench in the air. Tainted and stale.

He could also smell Rayna. Her scent hung heavy in the air and caused other parts of his body to ache. No matter what he did to chase her away, she was always there.

He'd been the biggest ass he knew how to be around her and still, she haunted him. Nothing he did got rid of her and he knew it would get her killed eventually, but staying away from her completely would only kill her faster. The body lying at his feet proved that fact. Thankfully Rayna hadn't been able to link all the victims together yet like he had. They all shared the same characteristics. He didn't even have to ask to know this woman was in her late twenties with brown hair halfway down her back, wore a size six, and had graduated from Hamilton College.

Just like Rayna. Just like all the victims.

The sound of footsteps caught his attention and he turned his head, watching his partner, Chad, approach him.

"Is she gone?"

"Yes. Less than three minutes," Garrett said, looking back down at the body. "Reynolds still tailing her?"

"Yeah."

"Good. Tell him not to let her leave his sight until I tell him otherwise."

"And how long will that be?"

"Until we catch whoever is doing this," he said, nodding his head toward the body.

"You know if the Chief finds out you're having her followed he'll have all our asses in a sling."

"Then I suggest you cover your tracks so he doesn't find out. She's in danger whether anyone wants to believe it or not."

"Is that the only reason you have her on twenty-four hour surveillance?"

Garrett looked up and frowned. Chad's faced was alight with laughter and a twinkle of amusement shined in his eyes. "I broke it off with Rayna for a reason, Chad."

"A reason you've yet to explain."

"I don't have to explain my actions to anyone."

"No, you don't, but any fool can see you're in love with her, which begs the question, why in the hell did you break up with her."

Garrett scowled and turned, walking away from the victim and from the truth Chad had so eloquently stated. Eight months of lying to every person he knew and not a one of them believed him. No matter how many times he denied it, his friends saw through his carefully constructed lies. Did Rayna? Did she know the very sight of her caused his chest to ache and his body to respond as if she'd touched him? That her scent stayed with him for days and he lost sleep as he watched her silent, dark apartment just to make sure she was safe?

No. She couldn't know. He purposely treated her like dirt anytime he saw her. Why would she know he was in love with her? How could she know that leaving her tore his soul into a thousand pieces and caused the wolf residing within his flesh to try and claw its way free to claim her as his own.

Two

"How do werewolves sound for our next big story?"

Rayna turned her head at the sound of Mitch's voice. Her newsroom partner for the last two years apparently had the nose of a bloodhound. The fact he'd found her tonight proved it. As usual, his suit was crisply starched and his light brown hair was arranged perfectly. Of course, a few unruly wisps curled around his ears and made him look years younger than he actually was but it didn't detract from his appeal. He was nice looking, in that boy next door kind of way. He slid onto the stool next to her and she raised an eyebrow at him. "Werewolves? I'm not writing for the trash mags, Mitch."

He laughed. "Neither am I. I'm serious."

"Oh, of course you are," she said, waving her hand to dismiss his comment. "Werewolves are all the craze nowadays." She smiled when the bartender slid her drink in front of her and she took a sip while Mitch ordered one of his own. "So, how did you find me?" she asked.

"It wasn't that hard." He stood when the bartender handed him his drink. He nodded at an empty table with his head before crossing the bar. Rayna followed him, pausing to let a group of giggling girls pass before sliding into the booth. "I had Daniels follow you when you left the office."

Rayna grinned and turned her head, scanning the crowded bar. "I didn't see him."

"He ducked out after calling me."

"Figures," she said, taking a sip of her rum and coke. "So, what was so important that you had to track me down for it?"

"Your friend Malcolm St. John sent you a package."

Rayna groaned. "Great. And here I thought my shitty day couldn't get any worse." Mitch pulled a yellow envelope out of his jacket pocket and she rolled her eyes before holding out her hand.

When he handed it to her, she saw her name scrawled across the front in elegant script and, in the top left hand corner, the name Malcolm St. John. Just the sight of his name left a bad taste in her mouth. Seven months of his harassing phone calls, a new telephone number and a restraining order later and he still insisted upon finding ways to contact her to tell his story. A story he'd yet to divulge. All she ever got from him was, "Come visit us and I'll make you famous."

Sighing, she shook her head and look down at the package. "I'm almost scared to look," she said. "This man is starting to be a serious pain in my ass." Knowing Mitch wouldn't leave until he'd seen what Malcolm's latest scheme was, she flipped the envelope over.

The tape was already ripped off. She raised her eyes and stared at Mitch.

"What?" he said, grinning. "I only had a peek."

"At my personal mail!"

The Calling

He snorted a laugh and nodded his head to the envelope. "Maybe, but that's not important at the moment. Malcolm's bizarre behavior just got interesting. Take a look."

Rayna emptied the envelope, laying the contents on the table. There wasn't much in it. A single sheet of paper and three photographs. Her eyes widened when she got a look at one of the photos. "Well, the man has a sense of humor at least," she said, reaching for one. "That's reassuring."

The first photo showed a man in some sort of spasm. He was on the ground, his body contorted in pain. He was naked, his back to the camera, and Rayna could barely make out the rigid protrusions along his spine. Bony shards stuck out from under his skin. He looked ghastly white, one arm outstretched as if asking for help.

The next showed the same man only this time, his body was covered in a thin layer of dark hair. The side of his face was visible. The forehead looked wider, his nose and mouth elongated and protruding from his face. His teeth were bared, sharp and gleaming in the moonlight. A shiny substance covering his skin seemed to glow in the filtered light.

The last photo showed the man on all fours, his neck outstretched and pointing to the sky. His mouth was open. The sharp teeth bared and something dripped from lips that no longer looked human. His eyes glowed brilliant yellow-orange, the hair along his body had thickened, the torso broader. His body still looked somewhat human but Rayna could tell something was happening to him. It looked like a shape-shift from any good horror movie she'd ever seen.

Why the photos were sent to her, she had no clue.

"What is Malcolm up to?" she asked. "A handful of fake pictures isn't going to lure me to him any quicker than his other attempts."

"Why do you automatically assume it's fake?" Mitch asked, reaching for the photos.

She laughed. "Uh, probably because werewolves don't exist, boy genius."

He threw her a look and sifted through the photos, examining each one carefully. She watched him for a few seconds before remembering the note that had accompanied the pictures and reached for it.

Dear Ms. Ford,

I've spent the last seven months trying to bring my community to your attention with no luck. I felt a little glimpse into what we have to offer was in order. I hope the photos will at least peek your interest enough to warrant a few minutes of your time. We are in desperate need of your help. Please reconsider my offer to visit us and let our story be known. I'll leave the communication between us up to you as you've asked me not to call. My number is on the back of the first photo.

Kindest regards,
Malcolm St. John

"Well, what does it say?"

"What? You didn't read it?"

He blushed and grinned at her. "No. Once I saw the photos the note didn't even dawn on me. So, what does he want?"

The Calling

"The same as always. The photos were just to peek my interest," she said, reaching for the pictures. "I'm not sure how this is relative to what he wants though."

"Well, he wanted your attention, Ford," Mitch said. "And I do believe he has it."

His laughter caused Rayna to roll her eyes. "I'm not that hard to impress, Mitch."

"Not in general, you're not," he said. "But when it's a story, you won't take anything but the best."

"You make that sound like a bad thing," she said, grinning. "We haven't won all those awards by taking on every piss-ass story that came along. Being selective is what's gotten me—us, where we are."

"True, but we haven't produced anything other than the serial killer in months."

"Oh, ye of little faith."

"Come on, Ford," Mitch said. "What's it going to hurt? The worst that can happen is we'll get a nice little vacation away from the city."

Rayna sighed. He was like this every time she heard from Malcolm.

"It's the perfect set-up," Mitch said. "We get paid downtime. Malcolm has practically begged you to tell his story."

"I don't care. I'm not doing it. Malcolm is crazy. Anyone who would stalk a reporter, just to have his name in the paper, can't be right in the head." Mitch's ears turned red then and Rayna narrowed her eyes at him. He wasn't telling her something. "What did you do, Mitch?"

"What makes you think I've done something?"

"Because your ears are red. You're lying to me about something. What is it?"

"My ears are red?" He lifted his hand, feeling his ear before looking at her.

"I can see it in your eyes, too. What did you do?"

He sighed and looked toward the bar. When she kicked him under the table, he yelled, "Ouch," before he turned his attention back to her. "Fine," he said. "I might have showed the pictures to a few people."

"What?" she said, panicked. "To who?"

He ducked his head and mumbled, "Clive."

Rayna's eyes widened. "Mitch!"

"I'm sorry," he said, looking up. "When I saw the envelope, I opened it. Clive walked by and saw the photos."

"This can't be happening." Rayna closed her eyes and took a deep breath. "Please don't tell me what I think you're going to." She opened her eyes when he didn't answer her and his cheeks reddened. "Damn it, Mitch! He wants me to go, doesn't he?"

"Yes. He said to tell you to take the case or else."

"Or else?" She had a very bad feeling all of a sudden. The look on Mitch's face only made it worse. "Or else what?"

He sighed and leaned across the table. "Come on, Ford, don't be so pissed. We haven't had anything worth reporting other than the Night Stalker in months. Harper's sorry excuse for a newspaper is selling faster than they can print them. Clive wants something to sell our paper."

Rayna laughed but there was nothing humorous about the situation. "Harper sells stories about alien's and demon spawned babies! That's not real news."

The Calling

"I know, but Clive said if that's what it took to get people to buy our paper, he'd print it."

Her head began to throb, a dull ache pounding between her eyes.

"Look, I'm sorry, okay?"

She shook her head. "Tell me that when we're surrounded by lunatics who think they can turn into werewolves."

He laughed. "Come on, Ford. Where's your sense of adventure?"

"This has nothing to do with adventure."

"Sure it does. You can't get more adventurous than werewolves."

"Werewolves don't exist, Mitch," she said, glaring at him.

"How do you know?"

She snorted a laugh. "Have you ever seen any roaming the streets?"

"No," he said. "And you won't either. If you were a supernatural creature of myth, one who people would fear if they knew you existed, would you really go around shouting to the world that you were one of the monsters."

"Mitch, there aren't any monsters in the world. It's make-believe crap they use to sell movies and books."

"Yes, but most of that *crap* is based on legend."

"It doesn't make it true."

"Maybe not, but this is still a great story."

"How so?"

"An entire town that thinks they're werewolves?" He laughed and tossed the picture down in front of her. "Think about it."

She did. She thought about her career going up in flames. She thought about being the laughing stock of the entire newsroom. She thought about hanging Mitch up by his toes and feeding him to rats. Very large rats.

"Look, I'm not asking you to believe, Malcolm," he said. "Just don't discount his claim because you *don't* believe him."

She was screwed. She could feel it like something sour in the bottom of her stomach. Her boss, Clive, would give her no choice in this. Pleading with him like she'd done in the past would be useless. Her instincts were dead on most of the time and something told her he wouldn't budge on this. She had no choice anymore. Crazy or not, Malcolm had sealed her fate with those damn pictures. "When does he want us to leave?" she asked.

"As soon as we can."

"Figures."

Mitch picked up the pictures again and looked through them before tossing them back in front of her. "Look, I have to go. Don't be pissed."

"Oh, I'm more than pissed," she said. "And you're going to pay for this dearly."

He laughed and stood up. "It's a date then, Ford. Just don't wait too long for my punishment."

She glanced up at him. "You're not going to enjoy it, Mitch."

"Sure I will," he said, grinning. "I get to go to work tomorrow and tell the entire office we're going away together. No punishment under the sun can diminish my delight in that."

The Calling

His laughter rang out over the noise of the nearby tables and a few people turned their heads to look. She watched him walk away before leaning back in her seat and staring down at Malcolm's letter again. "Malcolm, you clever old bastard, what the hell are you up to?"

She reached for the photos, examining each one in turn. They were taken in the woods from what she could tell. The man was sitting in a large dirt circle and trees surrounded him. She could see a few people in the background; eager looks on their faces.

Although she knew the pictures were a fake, she had to admit they looked pretty damn real. *Movie stills, maybe?* She flipped the pictures over. Kodak was printed on the back. "They could still have been printed off the computer," she said to herself.

Turning the pictures back over, she looked at each one again, trying to see if anything looked out of place. A movie camera or a light, maybe… something. There wasn't anything other than the man and the people in the background.

Looking at the people in the pictures, she focused her attention on each one. Did all these people think they were werewolves and if so, what would cause them to think it? Mass delusion? She sighed. Mitch was right about one thing. Werewolves or not, she had a story here. This many people thinking something so absurd was a reporters dream.

Glancing up when the sound of feminine giggles caught her attention, her heart nearly stopped when she saw Garrett and a group of his detective buddies make their way to the bar.

As always, his very presence made the room seem smaller. The air seemed to thicken and her pulse raced as she watched him. He was dressed in jeans and a long sleeve, light blue shirt, the material clinging to his muscled arms and chest. He looked damned fine in her opinion. That panty-melting smile of his flashed as he ordered a drink. She knew he'd asked for a beer without even hearing him. Bud Light in a long neck bottle, ice cold. That's how he liked them.

She sighed and leaned back in her seat. Why the man still affected her like she was a teenager with a crush was beyond her. Just the sight of him made her want to throw herself at him and damn the consequences. The fact he'd thrown her away like yesterday's garbage didn't even diminish the effect he had on her. Sure it hurt like hell but she couldn't get her fickle heart and her stubborn brain to agree on anything when it came to him. Asshole that he was, she couldn't stop wanting him.

A young blonde slid into the seat next to him and he flashed her a smile that spoke of things she'd no longer have. It caused her stomach to cramp. Painfully. The girl said something to him and when he laughed and leaned down to whisper into her ear, Rayna turned away, staring down at the table. Eight months since he'd broken up with her and not a day went by that she didn't think about him and even though he didn't ever have a kind word for her, she searched him out just to see him. Being in this particular bar was proof of that. She was a glutton for punishment, apparently.

She took a long sip of her drink and tried not to look back over at him, staring at the pictures in her hand instead. Maybe Malcolm's invitation wasn't such a bad idea after all. Bluff's Point was a small town and running into Garrett on a weekly basis was enough to cause even the sanest of people to go daft. Why she still wanted him after the way he treated her was a mystery she'd never figure out but watching him flirt with someone else tore her heart out.

Glancing back over at him, and watching him laugh with the unknown woman, sealed her fate. She had to get out of this town. Away from him. Her heart could only take so much.

Lifting Malcolm's note, she read it again and looked on the back of the pictures until she found the phone number. Grabbing her cell phone, she slid out of her seat and started for the back of the bar, trying to find a quiet place to talk.

She didn't see Garrett's gaze follow her through the crowded bar.

"Please tell me you didn't know she was going to be here?"

"Of course he did," Chad said, laughing. "Why else would he be out on a Friday night?"

"Fuck off, both of you," Garrett said, turning his head and staring down at the beer bottle in his hands. Like most Friday nights, he watched Rayna's apartment himself and usually did so alone, but the minute he saw her leave, dressed in tight jeans and a shirt that barely covered her ample breasts, he'd followed her to the same bar he'd met her in the night he ended up back in her apartment. He immediately called Chad. He knew if he walked in there alone and found her with someone, he'd lose it. His buddies were just there for protection.

Protection for whatever asshole tried to make the moves on his girl.

He was relieved to see her alone but he wasn't stupid enough to think she'd stay that way. Since the day he broke it off with her, he'd been waiting. Waiting for someone who wasn't him to get close to her. Someone who didn't insult her every chance they got like he did. Someone who could be with her and not get her killed, but much to his surprise, she hadn't seemed interested in dating again, which was just as well. He was sure half the town would know his secret if that ever happened. Regardless of how much control he had over his beast, the wolf would show itself to stake its claim. A claim he'd wanted to make the first time he held her, the first time she came with his name on her lips and caused the wolf to demand more.

A claim he couldn't make without running the risk of infecting her.

"Why don't you just go kiss and make up?" Chad asked. "It's obvious you want to."

"Not that simple," Garrett said. "Besides, what I want doesn't necessarily mean I can have it."

"And why is that? What's stopping you? Are you that damn scared of commitment?"

Garrett barely kept from growling. He felt his vocal cords vibrate and cleared his throat before turning to look at his friend. "I'm not scared of anything."

"Then why? I don't get it. Explain it to me."

"I don't have to explain it," Garrett said.

The Calling

"Explain it anyway."

He clenched his jaw and stared down at the bar. "It would never work, Chad. A year from now, maybe two, we'd be over, and all the shit in-between would have been for nothing. There's no reason to prolong the inevitable."

"So, you know it won't last for years so you just ended it?"

Garrett picked up his beer and took a long swallow. "Something like that," he said, staring at his reflection in the mirror above the bar.

Chad laughed. "That's the craziest shit I've ever heard, man. While most men hit it until it does go bad you drop her before it does. What planet are you from?"

"The one where I don't use people I care about." He turned his head, searching the back of the bar for her. He spotted her moments later, near a darkened corner on the phone. She was smiling, her thick locks spilling over her shoulders and running down her back. His cock twitched just looking at her. The wolf still wanted her. He still wanted her. Wanted her to the point his bones ached and his teeth itched to sink into her flesh. To feel her blood coat his tongue as he swallowed her essence and marked her body and soul as his.

She hung up the phone and tucked it into her back pocket before weaving her way through the crowded bar. Garrett didn't miss the looks she got as she passed by the men in her path. His chest rumbled as he watched them stare at her, saw them smile and whisper. Thankfully she was oblivious. As she neared him, he could tell she knew he was there. She was watching the floor as she walked, avoiding all eye contact with the bar. He ran an appreciative glance down her body, watching her hips sway as she walked before looking back up at her breasts. They swelled above the scooped neck of her blouse. He knew the weight of them, how they felt against his flesh, against his tongue, and he barely contained a growl of approval at the sight of her. When her scent hit him, he ground his teeth together, balling his hands into a fist to keep from reaching for her as she passed him.

"Hey, Rayna! Join us for a drink."

Garrett turned and looked at Chad when he yelled out to her and wanted to kill him where he sat. What the fuck was he doing? He saw Rayna out of the corner of his eye and took a deep breath before turning his head to her.

She stopped, met his gaze once before turning her head and smiling at Chad. "Detective Burrows," she said. "I'm not sure hanging out with Bluff's Point's finest would be such a good idea. It might give all the other reporters in town the wrong idea."

"Let them talk," Chad said, waving a hand to dismiss her comment. "What's the worst they can say?"

"Oh, that's an easy one," Garrett said, turning in his seat to face her. "That she slept her way through the department just to get a front page headline. By the way, didn't I see your name there today?" He felt like the lowest shit in the world the moment the words were out of his mouth, especially when she turned those big blue eyes on him. For whatever reason, today was the day she let his usual barbed comments affect her. He saw it shining in her eyes moments before her bottom lip trembled. She glanced at the blonde sitting next to him before looking back at Chad.

The Calling

"Thanks for the invite, but I'll have to pass. Excuse me, gentlemen."

And without even a glance in his direction, she turned and walked away. When the door closed behind her, Garrett waited a full five minutes before getting up and following her.

To his surprise, she was still in the parking lot, just sitting in her car, staring out the windshield. As he neared her, he saw the tears falling down her cheeks.

"Fuck." He sighed, his chest aching to the point of pain before weaving through the parked cars toward her. She saw him before he reached her and started the car, wiped her face dry and pulled out of the parking space, nearly running him over. The last thing he saw was her arm reach out the car window and her middle finger raise as she pulled out onto the road.

Three

"Just go ahead and admit it," Rayna said, grinning. "We're lost."

"We're not lost," Mitch growled, snatching the roadmap from her lap.

"Yes, we are," Rayna said. "We've been driving for over an hour and there's nothing here. Just trees and…" She looked out the window and made a small sound in the back of her throat. "Well, just trees." The car suddenly veered and she sucked in a harsh breath, her entire body clenching until Mitch gained control and steered them back onto the road. She glared at him when he grinned and made an apology. He was trying to drive and read the map at the same time. *Typical.* She sighed, shifting in her seat again to try and get comfortable.

The entire trip was a whirlwind of planning that she'd spent half the night preparing for. Clive had been thrilled when she called him at home and told him she'd take the case. Of course, he wasn't too happy about her leaving immediately. And neither was Mitch. She'd ruined his big triumphant dance around the office while he gloated about them going away together. When he'd asked what her hurry was, she'd lied and told him the sooner she could expose Malcolm for the conniving little troll he was, the sooner her life could get back to normal.

The Calling

Malcolm had been a pain in her ass for the better part of the year and if giving in and making an appearance in his little town was all it took to stop his harassment, then she'd do it.

No one needed to know Garrett, and his refusal to be civil with her, was the real reason.

She'd left the bar the night before a total mess. Watching him flirt with the blonde and then have his hateful words thrown at her had nearly killed her. Seeing him follow her to the parking lot, she'd been half tempted to just run him over but the fear of actually hurting him made her sick. Not that he had any of the same qualms. Hurting her seemed like his new life mission. Why that was still baffled her. He's the one who broke it off between them. If anything, she should be the one throwing hateful words at him, not the other way around. It was almost as if he went out of his way to offend her at every turn and no matter how hurtful his words were a small part of her was just grateful he was still talking to her. Just seeing him made her pulse race and caused her belly to ache. She missed the stupid jerk. Missed the way his arms felt around her and the way he smelled of earth and things alive and fresh. She missed his kisses and the things he said to her in the dark, of feeling safe and protected.

As pathetic as it was, she was still crazy about the asshole.

She shook thoughts of Garrett away before she once again slipped into pity mode and focused her attention on Malcolm, and the trip, and pushed Garrett to the back of her mind where he needed to stay. She knew this excursion was going to be interesting, regardless of her own personal beliefs of what was really happening in the mountain community of Wolf's Creek. After calling Malcolm herself, and the little speech her boss, Clive, gave her, she knew she had no excuse but to take the case seriously and do a proper story. She still wanted to laugh at the ridiculousness of it all, though. Werewolves. Honest to God, shape-shifting humans. The idea alone was preposterous.

In all her years as an investigative journalist she'd yet to come across anything as bizarre as this.

Of course, she knew the claim was false. There weren't any werewolves in the world but the story was still interesting. An entire town, living with the belief that they could all shift their shapes into something else was just… well, it was a goldmine is what it was. Mass delusion. And it was a delusion. She did find that piece of information during her Internet search the night before. A rare disorder referred to as Lycanthropy. A condition that caused its victims to believe they could shift their shape into other creatures. In this case, werewolves. She almost felt sorry for them. The reporter in her was eager for the story, damn the consequences. The human side pitied them.

The car slowed and Rayna glanced out the window. A town sprang up from nowhere amongst the trees and she turned her head to Mitch when he slowed the car and pulled up next to the curb. He was grinning from ear-to-ear.

"I told you we weren't lost."

The urge to stick her tongue out at him was great, but she refrained. She did roll her eyes before sitting up straight in her seat and peering out the window at the town. It looked to be exactly one street and they were on it. The sidewalk stopped a block down and turning to look behind her, she was met with the same sight. "Are you sure this is it, Mitch?"

"Yes, I'm sure," he said.

"Well, where's the hotel then?"

"That, I'm not sure of."

He turned the car off and opened his door, stepping into the deserted street. "Hello! Is anyone here?"

Rayna watched him walk a few feet from the car and yell again before she looked at what was supposed to be a town. There were exactly eight buildings on the right side of the road and seven on the left. A single stoplight hung from a line crossing the street. She'd thought Bluff's Point was small but this made the seaside community she'd called home all her life look like a bustling metropolis.

She opened her door and stepped out of the car. A glance at Mitch told her he was as puzzled as she was. They were in the heart of what looked like a ghost town. The place was deserted. There were no people milling around. The stores were all closed. Not a sound to be heard other than the wind and the noise the stoplight made as it swung across the street. It was almost spooky and the eerie feeling she was getting didn't bode well for the trip. "Are you sure this is it?" she asked.

"Yes, for the second time."

His curt reply left no room for argument and she sighed before walking around the car and stopping. She looked down the street in both directions before crossing her arms under her breast and leaning back against the car. "Okay, so what now?"

"I have no clue." He stepped up onto the sidewalk and peered into one of the shop windows, cupping his hands on the glass to block the suns glare. "It looks like a clothing store," he said. "But there's no one inside."

"Well, it is Sunday," Rayna said. "Maybe they're just closed."

A noise from behind them caused Rayna to jump before she swiveled her body to look. A man stood in the middle of the road staring at them. She gasped at his sudden appearance and unconsciously took a few steps backwards. "Where the hell did he come from," she whispered.

"Ms. Ford?"

Rayna stared at the man when he said her name and nodded her head when Mitch stepped closer to her. Her heart thudded in her chest and she took several deep breaths to try and control her breathing. "I'm Rayna Ford."

The man was tall and thin. His graying hair was cut short to his head and he wore a suit jacket with jeans and cowboy boots. He smiled and started toward them. "I'm Stan Buchanan. Welcome to Wolf's Creek."

"Uh, thanks," she said.

"We were expecting you earlier. Did you have trouble finding us?"

She smiled and glanced at Mitch. "A little," she said.

"Well I'm sure Malcolm will be happy to see you've arrived."

She nodded her head at him and took a quick glance around town. "It's kind of quiet around here, isn't it?"

The Calling

He laughed, the sound soft and warming. "We're pretty laid back here most of the time," he said. He walked toward them and stopped just behind the car. "And it's Sunday. None of the stores are open. If you need something I can make arrangements for you."

"We're fine," she said. "We have everything we need." Movement out of the corner of her eye caught her attention and she turned her head, looking to the opposite side of the street. A young boy stood in the shadows, watching them. "So," she said, "Where is everyone? The town looks a bit deserted."

"Oh, the others will be along shortly. We don't get many visitors here but I'm sure half the town knows you've arrived by now."

"One does," she said, nodding her head to the boy. When Stan turned his head to look at him, the boy ran around the corner of the building and was gone.

Stan smiled. "That would be Jacob," he said. "He's quite curious. As everyone will be."

"I see."

"When you're ready, I can show you to Malcolm's. You'll be staying at his home while you're here in town. I wish we could offer you more privacy but as you can see, we don't have public lodging."

"All I need is a place to lay my head," Mitch said, walking around the car and opening his door.

"Well, that we can offer you," Stan said. "Come. I'll take you to Malcolm."

Garrett looked up when Dan Reynolds stopped in front of his desk. He raised an eyebrow at him and leaned forward in his chair. "Why are you standing in front of me instead of watching Rayna?"

"Probably because I can't follow her past the county line," Reynolds said. "I figured you could so that's why I'm here."

"County line? She left Bluff's Point?"

"Yeah and she wasn't alone."

Garrett bit his tongue and took a deep breath. He stared across his desk at Reynolds and tried to calm his breathing.

"She left with Mitch Pierson…" Garrett could tell there was more in the way Reynolds paused. He waited, holding his body still and hoped like hell his face didn't reveal all he was feeling. The thoughts of Mitch and Rayna together caused the wolf to rage and beat against his flesh.

"I watched her pack suitcases into the back of Mitch's car," Reynolds said, "and then followed them all the way to the Interstate. They were headed south."

Garrett ground his teeth together, listening to the small crunch they made as his jaw tightened. Why this information surprised him, he didn't know. Mitch had never made it a secret he would help Rayna forget all her troubles, and him, and so far she'd acted as if she wasn't interested.

Apparently she's changed her mind. *And do you blame her after the stunt you pulled last night?*

Forcing himself to stay seated and not run straight to his truck and chase her down, he stared at his computers black monitor. "They were headed south? You're sure?" he asked, ignoring the roaring inside his head. How could he protect her if she wasn't there? If she wasn't there, he didn't need to protect her, did he? If he didn't need to protect her, then why was his wolf sliding against his bones and trying to get out? *Because your mate is with another man. A man that isn't you.*

"Yeah, south on I-95."

Garrett looked up and nodded, waving his hand and dismissing Reynolds. He waited until he was on the other side of the room before reaching for his keyboard. A few clicks and several minutes later, he pulled up the DMV records on Mitch and wrote down every piece of information he could find. The desire to have them stopped was strong but without a damn good reason he could do nothing.

He sighed and ran his fingers through his hair. Damn it, why did he have to push her buttons every time he saw her? Why couldn't he just let it go? He didn't have to prove to anyone, especially her, that he was over her. Surely she knew he was by the way he treated her but the fear she'd see through his lies was always there. Fear that she'd realize he only tormented her to remind himself he couldn't have her. That in alienating her, she'd hate him as much as he hated himself.

His phone rang and tearing his gaze from the computer, he answered. "Kincaid."

"Hello, lover."

Garrett's heart skipped a beat before his blood resumed rushing through his veins. He'd know that richly accented voice anywhere. He swallowed the instant rage that clouded his vision and caused his stomach to clench in dread and tried to keep his voice calm. "Carmen," he said. "What do you want?"

"What, no hello? I miss you?" She laughed and the sound of it beat against his skin like daggers. "You'd think after this many years your hatred for us would have lessoned."

"It hasn't."

"Still refusing to accept what you are?" she asked. "You'll never be one of them, Garrett, why do you still torture yourself by pretending?"

His pulse was racing and the wolf was fighting his way to the surface. He could feel it with every syllable she uttered. "You have less than two minutes to explain what you want, Carmen."

She laughed again and flashes of her invaded his mind. Memories he'd buried and thought long forgotten. "I thought we could plan a little conjugal visit since our last meeting didn't go so well," she said. "It's been way too long."

"Not long enough for me."

"The pack needs you, Garrett."

He turned in his chair, putting his back to the room. "No, *you* need me and I'm not ready to play Alpha to that twisted little pack you have wrapped around your conniving finger."

Her laughter was filled with a small growling purr. There was a time when the sound of it caused his body to harden. Now, it left him seeing blood. Hers, as it spilled from her body. "The sooner you realize you belong to us Garrett, the happier you're going to be. You can't play human forever. Someone will eventually realize you're one of the monsters."

"Maybe," he said. "But until then, someone has to protect the humans from the real monsters."

"And who is going to protect you?"

"I don't need protection."

"Of course you do," she said. "You're a danger to yourself."

He sighed and glanced around him before lowering his voice. "What do you want, Carmen. I know you didn't call just to hear my voice."

"No. I called to invite you home."

"Sorry. I'm not interested. Thanks for calling."

"Don't hang up!" she yelled.

His fingers twitched to do just that. The fact he was even still talking to her pissed him off.

"I have something of yours," she said. "I thought you might want to come and get it."

"There's nothing there that belongs to me, Carmen."

"Oh? I wouldn't be so sure of that," she said.

He could hear the rustling of fabric and her heels clapping against the floor before voices started filtering into the receiver. The harsh laughter of multiple voices reached his ears and he strained to hear what was being said. When the noise grew, he waited impatiently until he heard Carmen speak. "I'm sorry I missed your arrival. I was on an important business call. I'm Carmen Ortiz. You're Rayna Ford, correct?"

At the mention of her name, Garrett's wolf slammed against his bones hard enough to make him gasp. He felt it pulsing under his skin and when he heard Rayna's voice over the phone, his nails lengthened before he could stop it.

The connection died before he could even open his mouth.

That fucking bitch. I'll kill her. He could already taste her blood and his beast howled inside his head as he slammed the phone down and stood up. He was out the door and headed to his truck before he realized he was being set up. Carmen had lured Rayna there just like she was luring him. Rayna was the bait she waved at him to get him to finally come home. The bait she tried to kill to force him to give up his life and conform to her ways. When Carmen couldn't kill her, she forced him to come to her.

It was her last mistake. He'd see to that. So Carmen wanted her Alpha male back bad enough to risk her own life? He'd show her the error of her ways as he ripped her heart out and fed it to her one piece at a time.

Four

Rayna smiled as Carmen introduced her to yet another person she wouldn't remember the next day. A barrage of faces had greeted her since the moment they pulled up the long winding drive to Malcolm's home. The three-story house had sprung up out of the trees like some gothic monolith. The façade was covered in gray stone, large columns held up the second story balcony that spanned the entire front of the house. It looked out of place. Surrounded by trees, the structure was better suited for a windswept cliff overlooking a tide of raging sea. The interior hadn't diminished her observations. Dark, hardwood floors and heavy fabric drapes caused the rooms to have a dark, sinister feeling to them. She'd been uneasy since stepping foot inside the foyer. More so when she'd seen the first curious eye look her way.

The residents of Wolf's Creek had filled the house for the better part of an hour. They watched her, their faces neutral, but something in their eyes caused goose bumps to pimple her skin. They stared unabashed, sizing her up, for what, she didn't know, but they still watched her to the point she felt uneasy. And that feeling only intensified when Carmen had introduced her to the man with blue hair, Caleb. Him, she would remember.

She glanced over at him again as he leaned against the wall and noticed him still watching her. If she lived another eighty years she'd never forget him. He'd shocked her so much when she first saw him, she could do nothing but stare.

He'd entered the room as if he owned it, his gait slow and confident and she'd been too surprised by his appearance to look away from him. He was tall and incredibly thin with short spiky hair in the most flamboyant shade of blue she'd ever seen on anyone's head. A pair of leather pants was his entire wardrobe unless you counted the black leather bracelets that covered both his wrists. Dark liner outlined pale blue eyes that shined like small crystals as he watched her. His feet were bare, as was his chest, and rings pierced both his nipples. A condescending smile was plastered on his face and he stared intently at her as he walked closer. The minute he reached her and stopped, the leer he gave her made her skin crawl. The way he was looking at her now made her want to run. Very fast.

She looked away, focusing her attention back on Carmen. She was still talking and Rayna didn't have a clue what she'd been saying. She'd have to ask Mitch. Lord knows he was hanging on to every word. He hadn't stopped drooling since the woman walked into the room. She couldn't really blame him though. Carmen was very remarkable looking. Tall and dark skinned with an accent that would turn any man's head. Her hair hung in silky waves down her back all the way to her hips and it was a black so dark, it looked almost blue under the lights. Her limbs were long and graceful and she had a body women would have to pay to have. In a word, she was breathtaking. She wanted to hate her for that fact alone but she wasn't catty... not usually, but she felt like a short, fat dumpling standing beside of her. Even Mitch barely noticed her and he couldn't go five minutes without saying something salacious to her.

Malcolm walked back into the room and once again, Rayna couldn't take her eyes off of him. He was not what she had been expecting.

To say she was shocked by his appearance would be an understatement. She'd spent months corresponding with him by phone or letters and like most people you only talk to but never see, she'd forged a mental image of him in her head. How wrong her imagination had been. She'd assumed he was some harebrained loon with wild eyes and hair to match and even a wilder personality. That isn't what she got at all. This man looked like he should be sitting at the head of some large corporation making million dollar deals. He appeared to be in his fifties, tall, and strongly built. He was quite distinguished looking and had an air of authority about him that she wasn't expecting.

He'd introduced himself and was so pleasing in personality the uneasy feelings she'd gotten when first arriving at the monstrosity of a house slowly began to ebb. If everyone in this town was under some sort of mass delusion, Malcolm included, they hid it well. Aside from the strange looks she'd been receiving, they all acted completely sane to her.

"Ms. Ford," Malcolm said when he reached her. "Stan has put your things in your room. I've placed Mr. Pierson in the room next to yours at your request. I'm sure you're tired from your trip so please, don't let us keep you from retiring. I apologize for monopolizing your time. We have so few guests here we get carried away and forget our manners."

She smiled and gave him a fake yawn. "That's quite all right," she said. "I've enjoyed the party but you're right, I am tired, but I wouldn't want to upset your guests by disappearing so early."

"Nonsense," he said, waving his hand to dismiss her comment. "They have all day tomorrow to meet you before our little presentation. Please, your rooms are ready whenever you are. Just take the stairs. Your rooms are at the end of the hall. The last two on the left."

Rayna glanced at Mitch and noticed he was still engrossed with Carmen. She wanted to laugh and tell him he didn't have a snowballs chance in hell with a woman like that but decided to let him find out on his own. Besides, what did she know? Carmen might make her friends millennium and give him a happy before they left. Stranger things had happened. She turned back to Malcolm and said, "I do believe I'll go on up. Thank you for the warm welcome. It wasn't necessary."

"Oh, but it was," he said. "You're going to be the salvation we've all been waiting for."

She wanted to question him about that but decided against it. She smiled at him and walked from the room, glancing at the blue haired Caleb out of the corner of her eye. For some reason, he was still watching her.

The Calling

The ritual grounds, as Malcolm had called it, wasn't anything more than a large dirt circle edged on three sides by massive trees. Rayna stopped by a large oak and sat her camera bag down, taking it all in. Majestic pines perfumed the air with the fresh, clean scent, their branches swaying in the wind. A sheer rock face marked the fourth boundary. The boulder was massive and looked out of place. There were small protrusions carved into it, jutting from the face making what looked to be some sort of seating shelf. This far up on the mountain the air was cool and she wished she'd brought a jacket. She was sure once the sun set, she'd be sorry she hadn't.

A glance into the sky showed the purple and orange hues of the setting sun. The area inside the circle was lit only slightly more than that of the surrounding woods. She was glad there would be a full moon tonight. Her camera flash would disturb whatever Malcolm had planned for them. She just hoped the moon illuminated the area enough to be able to take her pictures without the need for a flash.

She saw Malcolm enter the circle and watched him for long minutes as he smiled and talked with a few people she met at the house the night before. When he'd joined them for breakfast, he'd been secretive about what exactly it was he wanted to show her. Her questions about his werewolf claims went unanswered despite her numerous attempts to engage him. He'd smiled and made small talk throughout the day, giving her a brief history on their little town, giving her a tour of his massive, three story home, but nothing more. He said, "she'd find out soon enough," and left it at that.

Malcolm was, in essence, the perfect host, but something sent a trickle of unease up her spine as the day went by. Mitch had felt it too. They had been watched curiously by everyone. More so than the night before. Every person they encountered looked too eager for them to be there. Their smiles were too wide. They were treated like royalty and that alone sent up warning flags. Something was about to happen and for some reason, Rayna didn't think she was going to like it. Story or not, tonight would change her life. She felt it to the marrow of her bones.

"So, what do you think we've gotten ourselves in to?"

Rayna looked up at Mitch when he spoke. His thick, brown mane of hair was disheveled and she raised an eyebrow at him. "We? You were the one who got us in to this mess."

He grinned. "Maybe. Clive would have been on our ass eventually, anyway. Besides, we have a story no matter what these people do. Everyone we've met is strange."

"Strange doesn't even begin to describe it," she said. "The woman at the house today... what was her name? Judy...no, Judith! Judith said we were to witness a mass shift."

Mitch snorted a laugh. "So they really do believe they're werewolves?"

"Apparently so."

"Well, we're in for an interesting night then."

"Yes, but for some reason, although I know their claim is bogus, I get the feeling there's more going on here."

The Calling

"How so?"

She shrugged one shoulder. "I can't explain it," she said. "Most everyone I met today kept looking at me funny."

"Well, you aren't that horrible on the eyes, you know."

Rayna looked up, watching him glance down the line of her body and give her a leer that should have flattered her. It didn't. She reached out and smacked him on the arm. "Stop trying to change the subject."

"I'm not," he said. "You look quite scrumptious tonight."

"Geez. I'm not going to have to put up with you too, am I?"

"Maybe," he grinned.

"Go make yourself useful and find out what these people are up to."

"Fine, but grab every picture you can. I'd like to be out of here by sunrise. This place is starting to give me the creeps."

"Same here." She watched him walk away, heading for a small group that was gathered by the rock.

Kneeling down, she opened her camera bag, pulling out her equipment and readying her camera. She sat the bag by a large tree and spent the next several minutes snapping shots of the area.

She concentrated on the people gathered, snapping pictures of individuals and then groups.

From the looks of it, there were more than forty people in the area already. She wasn't sure how many people lived in Wolf's Creek but with each new face, her story became more interesting. Had this many people ever been under the same mass delusion at the same time?

Turning, she snapped shots of more people coming from the woods, zooming in on their faces as they cleared the dark interior of the forest. When the slow traffic of bodies stopped moving, she lowered her camera.

The sky was darkening, the first twinkling of stars shining through the small opening in the trees and she stared in wonder at the sky. Everything was so clear here. You didn't see a sky like that in the city. The only sounds she could hear were the low, whispered conversations going on around her and the chirping songs of crickets. It was peaceful but she knew it wouldn't stay that way. Her weird-o-meter was clicking louder with every passing minute.

Commotion to her left brought her attention back to the gathering and she raised her camera, zooming in on the small group. Malcolm's presence seemed to excite the others. He looked damn near regal as he strolled into the circle. A smile beamed from his face and he greeted everyone who approached him while making his way to the rock face.

A sudden movement to the left of the crowd, just beyond the tree line startled her. She zoomed her camera in on the spot. Something darted past her and she lowered the camera trying to see what it was. The forest was too dark to see into with the naked eye.

The crackle and pop of branches behind her startled her and she turned, peering into the darkness at her back. Nothing moved and she strained her eyes to see if anyone was there.

The Calling

Garrett knew Rayna couldn't see him but the weight of her stare penetrated his skin. Tiny pinpricks danced down his arms and he froze when she took a step into the dark confines of the forest.

What moonlight shining on the area glowed behind her and outlined her body, casting a dark silhouette that defined her curves. His wolf beat against his skin suddenly, wanting to get closer. It prowled just below the surface and roared inside his head. He'd wanted to grab her the minute he saw her but he knew, with this many at the ritual ground, he was outnumbered. Besides, if he made himself known now, he'd never know what they were really up to.

He saw Malcolm just over Rayna's shoulder and when he spoke, she turned, putting her back to him. He moved then, edging closer to the tree line and stopped a few yards back.

The crackle of breaking branches startled him and he spun on his heel, crouching down and peering into the forest. He eased his stance once he saw who it was. "Do you have a death wish, pup?"

The boy's cheeks reddened. "No and I thought after all this time you would have outgrown that horrible nickname."

Garrett grinned. "You are what you are, Jacob." It had been twelve years since he'd left Wolf's Creek and Jacob hadn't aged a day. He still looked like the sixteen-year-old boy he found hiding in an abandoned cabin up on the ridge, living off rabbits and not much of anything else. The day he'd left Wolf's Creek, he'd begged Jacob to go with him. The boy refused saying he much preferred the mountain to the city. Reaching out, Garrett laid his hand on his shoulder. "How have you been?"

"The same," Jacob said. "Nothing changes around here."

"That much I can see. You're still an impulsively careless wolf. You shouldn't be sneaking up on me," he said, tightening his grip on Jacob's shoulder. "It's a good way to end up with your throat ripped out."

Jacob snorted a laugh and threw Garrett's hand off his shoulder. "You're just pissed because I was actually *able* to sneak up on you." He looked back to the circle and motioned toward it with his head. "I saw her come in yesterday and I overheard some of the others talking about her. I think some serious shit is about to go down. That why you decided to come back home?"

"Yes," Garrett said. "She's the only reason I'm here."

Jacob smiled and took a step closer to him. "She yours?"

Garrett wasn't sure how to answer that. His wolf screamed yes, but the human part of him knew he'd tossed her away. Given her up to protect her from his life. From the secret no one knew except the people he used to call family. The people who had lured her here.

"She looks young," Jacob said when he didn't answer.

Garrett nodded his head, watching her. "She's too old for you, Jacob."

Jacob growled softly and turned to him. "I'm twenty-seven, Garrett."

"Yes, but you look like you still need your ass powdered. But hey, what do I know? She might have some hidden kink for young boys."

Jacob laughed. "Fuck you, man."

Rayna moved into the circle. The light from the moon shined down on her and Garrett could see her clearly now. Her hair fell down her back in soft waves. Jeans and a black blouse hugged her like a second skin. His body tightened just looking at her. The fullness of her breasts, the curved perfection of her bottom, those impossibly long legs that used to wrap around his hips as he plunged into her. There wasn't another woman in all of Wolf's Creek who even came close to looking like that.

Well, no one but Carmen.

He'd seen that bitch the minute he entered the forest. Her scent caused the hair on the back of his neck to rise and forced a growl to rumble in his chest. She looked exactly the same as she did the day he left twelve years ago. Tall, statuesque, with straight black hair that brushed her hips as she walked. The desire to walk up to her and rip her heart from her conniving chest was great. The only thing that stopped him was Rayna. Insuring her safety was his main priority.

But no worries, he'd kill the lying bitch when Rayna was out of harms way.

Garrett leaned back against a tree and nodded to the circle. "Head on over there and see what's going on."

"You're not coming?"

"No."

"So what, I'm supposed to report back to you now? You've been back on the mountain less than a day and I'm your errand boy again?"

"No," Garrett said. "My senses are perfect. I can hear perfectly clear what's being said. You on the other hand, can't."

"And how do you know?"

"Because Malcolm's been asking where you are for the last five minutes."

Jacob's eyes widened before he sprinted toward the clearing. Garrett laughed and crossed his arms over his chest.

Rayna turned at the sound of someone running and watched a boy barrel his way into the clearing. He was stick thin but tall with a thick mass of curly blond hair that fell onto his forehead. He looked over at her as he walked past and she smiled at him. His cheeks reddened as he blushed. When he stopped in front of Malcolm, she lifted her camera, snapping a few shots of him.

"Judith, you come as well," Malcolm said.

When they were both in front of him, Malcolm turned to face her. "Ms. Ford," he said, then turned his head to Mitch. "Mr. Pierson. This is Judith and Jacob. They'll both be seeing to your needs while you are with us. If you need something during the duration of your stay, just ask. Anything we have is at your disposal."

The Calling

Rayna glanced at Mitch and raised an eyebrow at him. Apparently Malcolm expected them to stay longer than they intended. What would he do when they told him they were leaving in the morning?

When Judith walked over to her and Jacob approached Mitch, Rayna watched with interest as Malcolm headed to the large rock face and stepped up on the low shelf. It put him in a good position to be seen by everyone and she once again raised her camera and snapped a shot of him.

"We should move closer to the trees," Judith said. "It'll be safer there."

Rayna glanced at her. The woman was short and thin, her shoulder length hair was a dull, light brown. She wasn't sure her age but it was close to forty. The wrinkles around her eyes and mouth told her that much. "Okay," she said and turned, walking back to where her camera bag lay. She noticed Mitch walking toward her, his escort following close behind. When he stopped by her side, she leaned toward him. "We should have told Malcolm we weren't staying."

"He'll find out soon enough."

Looking toward Malcolm when he started talking, Rayna focused her attention on him.

"I'd like to thank Ms. Ford and Mr. Pierson for finally joining us. You have no idea how happy you've made us all."

Rayna forced a smile on her face when everyone turned to look at them. She felt instantly exposed and shifted on her feet.

"Now," Malcolm said. "The reason we've brought you here, Ms. Ford, is two-fold. The first, I've already mentioned although you don't believe me." He chuckled and turned to a man standing by his side, clapping him on the shoulder. "We'll remedy that shortly."

The man at Malcolm's side had wide shoulders and a head full of dark hair cropped close to his skull. He was nice looking but something in the way he walked spoke of a confidence his face didn't show. She hadn't seen him the night before at Malcolm's little get-together but something about him was familiar. The man walked to the center of the dirt circle and stopped, facing her and Mitch. She watched him remove his shirt, exposing muscles the typical man didn't possess.

"This is Bryce," Malcolm said. "He's the man in the photos I sent you."

Ah, Rayna thought, with a nod. *That's why he looks familiar. The werewolf.* She smiled and continued to watch.

"Bryce has agreed to once again give you a demonstration of what we are. Please, don't be frightened. No one here will harm you. Judith and Jacob will see to it."

Harm them? That got her attention. Her pulse quickened and she turned her head, glancing at the two people flanking her and Mitch. *These two skinny, weak looking humans were going to keep them safe? Safe from what, is a better question.* She turned back to Bryce, an uneasy feeling causing her stomach to ache all of a sudden. He was still looking at her and something in his eyes made her pulse start to race.

"For everyone else," Malcolm said, "Please refrain from shifting for as long as you can. We don't want to alarm our guest. Bryce, whenever you're ready."

The Calling

"What does he mean exactly by shift?" Rayna asked, looking away from Bryce.

"He's going to shift his shape," Judith whispered. "Don't be scared. It's a little frightening the first time you see it, so be prepared."

"You mean change into a werewolf?" Rayna raised her eyes to Mitch who was still watching the man in the circle. She could tell he was trying not to grin. His lips were pinched shut, the corners white from the pressure. She smiled and looked back at Judith. "Does everyone here think... uh, I mean, can you all shift into wolves?"

"Yes," she said. "We'll all be shifting tonight."

A glance up at the night sky showed a moon that glistened against a velvet black background. Small rings of light encircled it and the bright glow grew with each passing minute. "A full moon," she said quietly. "Why am I not surprised?"

Judith's giggles brought her attention back to her. "We don't need the moon to shift," she said, "regardless of what the movies say. But most everyone likes the ritual of the change. Shifting is a rebirth, so to speak, so scheduling that with the moons phases just seems natural."

Rayna bit her lip to keep from smiling. "So the full moon doesn't force the change?"

Judith shook her head. "No. We do need to shift on a regular basis or the beast gets restless. We just choose the night of the full moon because it brightens the earth. It makes our hunt easier."

"The hunt?"

"Yes. What else would wolves do besides hunt and mate?"

Judith's cheeks reddened and Rayna smiled. "So what," she said, "You all get together once a month, shift into werewolves and chase each other through the woods for a little furry sex?"

"It's not quite as bad as it sounds," Judith said, giggling, "but basically, yes. It's the one time a month we let ourselves go and just let nature run its course. We can't change at will like the Alpha's can so it's a big deal to us."

"Change at will?" Rayna asked.

"Yes. The Alphas, they can shift at any given time. Several times a month if they want. It's why they're so feared and respected. They have a power the Betas don't."

"What's a Beta?"

"Oh, it's just what we call the less important wolves. Pack society is arranged in classes. The Alpha's are the strongest; the Beta's are next. Most everyone is a Beta. We're looked upon as the submissive wolves. We do as the elder's request or as the Alpha's command. And then you have the Omega." She turned her head toward Mitch and the boy. "That would be Jacob. He's the Omega of our pack. He's the least threatening so most everyone sees him differently."

"So it's really all about power and who has it?"

Judith smiled. "Something like that, yes. The Beta's will never lead the pack or hold any influence over the others; only the Alpha's can do that. Beta's can only shift into full wolf and most of the time, only once a month. It's too painful otherwise. The Alpha's can shift effortlessly, though. They can shift to a half form, I guess you can call it. They still look somewhat human and stand erect but they're still wolves."

"And how many can do that?" Rayna asked, taking mental notes of everything.

"Only a handful in our pack. You'll be able to see the difference once everyone shifts."

"You're not shifting?"

Judith smiled. "I will later. Malcolm wishes us to remain in our human form until you're back at the house."

"I see," Rayna said. "So how long does it normally take? To shift, I mean?"

"It depends on the person," Judith said. "And how strong they are. I've seen Alpha's change in a less than a minute. Bryce is an Alpha but he isn't as strong as some so it'll take a little longer for him to shift."

Rayna stared at Judith as she explained werewolf society to her and just barely kept from laughing. These people really did believe they could shift their shape. She looked at those around the circle, watching their faces. They were all staring at Bryce. As crazy as they all seemed she felt sorry for them. What would cause this many people to believe such a thing?

What if it's real? What if they can *turn themselves into wolves?*

A rustle of leaves behind her startled her and Rayna turned her head, looking over her shoulder. She still couldn't see anything in the darkened forest but scanned the area for movement anyway.

"It's probably just stragglers," Judith said, turning and looking into the forest. "Malcolm gets angry when we're late. They're probably just hiding from him."

Rayna nodded her head and gave the area one last look before turning back to Bryce. He was still just standing there but he wasn't looking at them anymore. He was staring into the sky, his body completely still.

Leaning back against a tree, she raised her camera, snapping a few shots and checking to see if he was visible without the flash. She smiled at the results.

A sound similar to a low growl cut through the stillness of the circle and Rayna looked around her to see where it had come from before focusing her attention back on Bryce. His skin now glistened with beads of perspiration, dotting along his face and shoulders. His chest was rising, his breaths panted out quickly, and Rayna pushed away from the tree and took a step forward.

A loud howl sliced through the forest and she jumped, startled, her heart leaping in her chest. The other residents of Wolf's Creek were now moving closer to the circle. Some were shedding their clothes, stripping down naked, and she looked at Mitch to see if he'd noticed.

He did. The wild, glassy look in his eyes told her as much.

When the woman she'd met at the house the day before, Carmen, stepped to the front of the group and looked at her, grinning widely before stripping to nothing, Rayna could only stare wide-eyed. *What the hell is going on?* "Mitch?"

"Still here," he whispered.

She wanted to look behind her just to make sure but she couldn't look away from the scene before her.

The Calling

Something was definitely happening. The air seemed charged with some unknown force all of a sudden. It buzzed along her limbs and caused the hair on her arms to stand on end. Her pulse started to race and that uneasy feeling she'd had earlier multiplied ten-fold.

When Bryce tilted his head back and opened his mouth, the noise he made sent bolts of fear crawling up her spine. It sounded similar to a growl but a very human scream accompanied it. Her stomach clenched, the first hint of fear starting to worm its way inside her head and when Bryce lowered his head and looked at her, his eyes glowed bright amber. She gasped and took a step back. "What the hell," she whispered.

Mitch moved closer to her and laid his hand on her shoulder. His grip tightened when Bryce doubled over, his hands clutching his stomach as he let out another ear piercing scream. The noise echoed in the forest, noises that weren't human mixed with those pain-filled shrieks before what could only be described as a wolf's howl escaped his mouth. The others followed suit, those naked bodies closing in on the circle shining under the full moon and Rayna felt dizzy within seconds. "What the fuck is going on?"

"Don't be scared," Judith said. "Your fear will make things worse."

She turned her head to the woman. "My fear?"

"Fear is an aphrodisiac. It calls to the beast," she said.

Rayna looked back at the people gathered and noticed then that everyone was staring at her. She swallowed the sudden lump in her throat and willed her heart to stop racing.

"Wolves are dominating creatures," Judith said. "Your fear smells like food to us. Just relax. No harm will come to you." She smiled and Rayna could tell she was trying to calm her but it wasn't helping. Something was happening. What, she didn't know, but she wasn't naive enough to think this show they were putting on was as innocent as she first thought.

"He's shifting," Judith said. "Look."

Turning back to the circle, Rayna could only stare as Bryce hit his knees and screamed. Harsh, rasping noises escaped his throat and the sound sent chills racing along her limbs. His skin turned gray and waxy, his back arched while his neck stretched in a painful looking angle.

In a perfect parody of the photos she'd been sent, Bryce's body began to change, his skin stretched, bones moved beneath his flesh and expanded. His screams caused her heart to race out of control as a thick, clear fluid slid over his skin and dripped to the ground before the hair on his body grew thicker. His mouth and nose elongated and when he lifted his head and opened his mouth, she gasped as long, razor sharp teeth grew from his gums and gleamed in the light of the moon. Another howl tore through the forest, followed by a symphony of growls that caused her head to spin and her stomach to tremble.

Five

When Bryce no longer resembled a human, he lifted his head, looking at her through those glowing, amber eyes. Rayna stared at the wolf looking back at her. A wolf that had once been a man. She felt her knees go weak an instant before the world spun.

Mitch caught her before she hit the ground.

She couldn't speak. Her limbs felt like they weighed a ton and she was suddenly nauseated. Her heart raced and the blood rushing through her veins pounded inside her head. When Mitch laid her down, she stared up into the night sky.

"Damn it, Ford, don't do this right now! Come on, nice even breaths."

Rayna closed her eyes, concentrating on her breathing. *I'm not going to pass out. I'm not going to pass out. I'm not going to pass out.*

The mantra worked. The nausea passed after a few minutes. When she opened her eyes, Mitch was still there, his face void of color and his eyes as wild and frightened as she knew her own were.

Judith and Malcolm stepped into her line of sight and she could only stare up at them.

"Are you all right, Ms. Ford?" Malcolm asked.

She said, "yes," while shaking her head no. She blinked away tears and tried to get her heart to stop pounding. Looking back up at Mitch, she prompted him to help her up. When she was on her feet and knew she wasn't going to faint, she looked over at Bryce. He was still sitting where he had been, his large, amber wolf eyes gleaming with light. She swallowed to moisten her throat. "I didn't believe you."

Malcolm laughed, loud and boisterously. "I know you didn't, Ms. Ford. It's why I pushed so hard for you to come. No one believes until they see."

She nodded, locking her gaze on Bryce.

"The others feel the pull of the shift, Ms. Ford. Will you be all right to watch? I can have Judith escort you back to the house if you prefer."

"No," she said, her voice trembling. She cleared her throat and said, "No, I want to see."

Taking a deep breath she looked for her camera and picked it up once she spotted it. Her hands were shaking, her entire body was trembling, but she swallowed the fear and adjusted the camera's settings. Malcolm walked away, joining the others and the minute she raised her camera, low, multiple howls echoed through the forest.

It was a thing of nightmares as she watched, snapping pictures as fast as she could hit the button. Tears clouded her vision and she blinked them away and tried to remain calm. Instinct told her to run. To run as far and as fast as she could but that little part of her that left her dangerously curious wouldn't let her. She had to see. Had to have proof that this really happened. That she wasn't hallucinating. That there were people in the world that turned into creatures so frightening that she could barely look at them without screaming.

The others in the circle shifted, their bodies undulating as they shed their human forms. Hair appeared where slick skin once was, teeth that belonged to an animal gleamed and snapped, claws raked at the ground and with every new wolf she saw, her fear grew, clawed at her lungs until she fought for every breath as she tried to hold her camera still while snapping picture after picture.

Everyone looked different to some degree, she noticed. Some had the appearance of regular wolves, only larger. They were big; standing on all fours they resembled bears in size more than wolves. She'd never seen anything so big this close up nor had she ever seen anything so horrifying.

A few of the others were still on two feet. They looked more like wolf-human hybrids. They were tall, all reaching over six-foot with a thick coat of hair covering their bodies. She could see genitals on the men that still somewhat resembled a human penis only the large quantities of hair on their bodies hid the majority of them from view. The sight caused her cheeks to heat before she looked away. Wolves or not, they were still very much human. The few women in this form still had their breasts but just like the men, were covered by hair.

Her breath was panted out unevenly and when the last person in the circle shook their human form, a multitude of amber eyes turned toward them. "Why do I feel like I'm someone's dinner all of a sudden?"

Jacob moved then, placing himself in front of her, and even though he wasn't much larger than she was, she felt better having him there. "Thanks," she whispered.

"They don't mean you any harm. They just want you to see them. It's why you're here."

"Yeah. I see them," she said. "I'm just having a real hard time believing it."

"Ms. Ford," Malcolm said. He was at the rock again. He hadn't shifted. He still looked as he had earlier.

"Can Malcolm shift?" she asked.

"Yes. We all can."

The boy turned after answering her. He was so young. A child, really. Why was he even here? "Can you?" she asked.

He grinned. "Yes."

She stared at him for long moments. His cheeks reddened before he looked away and she turned her attention back to Malcolm when he spoke again.

"If you and Mr. Pierson would come forward, we'll get to the second reason I've asked you here."

The wolves in the middle of the circle parted, slinking back along the tree line and creating a wide path to the rock face. Mitch was the first to move and no matter how brave she wanted to be, Rayna found it hard to take that first step.

"It'll be all right," Judith said, laying a hand on her arm. "Go on."

Rayna looked at her and saw the smile on her face but something in her eyes made her pause. Judith averted her gaze before she could figure out what it was. When Malcolm said her name again, she swallowed the lump in her throat and hesitantly followed Mitch. When they stopped in front of Malcolm, she turned in a circle, looking at the multitude of amber wolf eyes staring back at her from the trees.

The Calling

When Malcolm spoke, she turned to face him.

"Most of us have lived here, secluded from the outside world, for the better part of thirty years," he said. "We'd like to change that, Ms. Ford. You can help us do that."

"How so?" she asked, watching one of the female wolves jumped up onto the rock shelf. She was on two legs, the hair covering her body black. She towered over Malcolm, her lips pulled back slightly, showing her teeth. For whatever reason, it was her she was snarling at. She looked back at Malcolm. He was still smiling. He looked younger suddenly, his eyes lighting up.

"We don't venture into the real world," he said. "Your world, that is. It isn't designed for us. As you just felt yourself, people will fear us. We don't want that."

"They will," Rayna said, trying to keep her voice from trembling. "You can't do what just happened here outside of this town. You'd be shot."

"We know. It's how we, the majority of the people you see around you today, came to be here to begin with." Malcolm stepped off the rock ledge and walked closer to them. "I, along with many of the people you've met here, were in the wrong place at the wrong time. We were attacked by a wolf exactly like the ones you see now. The year was nineteen seventy-seven. I was fifty two years old."

Rayna raised an eyebrow at him. "You don't look much older than that now."

He smiled. "We don't age the same as humans," he said. "It's one of the many pleasant side effects of a Lycanthrope. I'm eighty three, or will be in four months."

Rayna gaped at him and shut her mouth when she realized it was open. She glanced at Mitch and saw he'd had the same reaction.

"We want the world to know we exist, Ms. Ford. Will you help us?"

"Help you? How?" she asked.

"By showing them what they thought to be only legend, or stories of monsters, are true."

Rayna laughed. "People will think I'm as crazy as I thought you were if I print a story claiming werewolves really exist."

"You'll prove it to them."

She smiled and raised her camera. "Malcolm, no one is going to believe these pictures. Have you seen any werewolf movies lately? What just happened here looked damned close to most movies I've seen."

"Then there are shifters in Hollywood," he said, grinning. "We're many in number, Ms. Ford. Our small pack is only one of thousands throughout the world. We've been in hiding since the dawn of time. We grow weary of doing it any longer. We just need a spokesperson to bring us into the light. They'll believe you, Ms. Ford. Please, tell our story."

"What makes you think that?" she said. "I'm no one, Malcolm. Just a reporter."

"People know you. They recognize your face and your name. Once they see, they'll have no reason not to believe you."

He looked over her shoulder and Rayna turned her head. The circle of wolves around them was getting smaller. They were slowly moving closer. Her fear escalated then. She had a really bad feeling. Turning back to Malcolm she said, "What exactly do you want me to do?"

He smiled and inhaled deeply, letting it out in a slow, hushed breath. "It's simple, Ms. Ford. Once you return to the city, tell our story."

"They won't believe me."

"But they will," he said. "When you shift for them, they'll believe you."

"Shift?" she said, her eyes widening. "But I can't shift..." The minute the words were out of her mouth she knew what his plan was. Why he'd tried so hard and so long to get her to visit him. The multitude of amber wolf eyes watching her, and the funny looks she'd been getting all day, now made perfect sense. Her heart slammed against her ribcage and she felt her lunch start crawling back up. Tears burned the back of her eyes as she stared at him. *Oh god, please let me be wrong.*

The group of wolves behind Malcolm was slowly making their way toward them. Her fear spiraled out of control and caused her vision to blur as her blood raced through her veins. She heard it gushing past her ears as she raised her eyes, meeting Malcolm's gaze and took a step back. "Malcolm?"

His smile dimmed but the sparkle in his eyes remained. "It will only hurt for a moment, Ms. Ford. I promise."

When the first tear fell she shook her head and said, "No..." She took a step back and remembered the wolves at her back. A glance over her shoulder confirmed they were still there and were advancing.

"It's just a small bite."

"No!" she said, taking four quick steps to the side, back toward the tree and her path to freedom. "Mitch!" She searched for him, seeing him to Malcolm's left. He looked frozen. His complexion was ashy, his eyes impossibly wide. He was being surrounded.

When Malcolm turned his head to look at Mitch and nodded, the wolves attacked him. Mitch's frightened scream sliced through her skin like hot pokers. The fear crawling up her throat choked her but when she saw Mitch fall, the wolf leaning over him with blood dripping from its teeth, she screamed, dropped her camera, and ran for the trees.

Garrett raced toward the circle and stepped from behind the trees. Rayna screamed again and slid to a stop, her eyes wide when she saw him. He caught her in his arms, spinning her around and placing her against a tree. "Don't move! You run and they'll kill you faster, got it!" He didn't wait for her reply, instead, he turned back to face the pack and took a step backwards, placing her completely behind him. She was wedged between him and the tree. They'd have to move him to get to her and that wasn't going to happen.

Lowering his arm, he grabbed her hand to keep her from running. Her nails bit into his flesh and he felt her trembling against his back, her harsh sobs and the scent of her fear forcing his beast to the surface. It was a struggle to keep it restrained. He felt it beating against his skin, struggling to be free. He let out a low warning growl, watching as those in pursuit slowed before coming to a stop.

"Look who decided to come home." Caleb walked closer, lifting his head to sniff the air. "You still smell like a coward to me, Garrett. Let her go and I'll let you live."

Garrett crouched low ready for an attack. "Not likely, Caleb. You can't do this."

"We can and we will."

Caleb's voice was distorted in wolf form and Garrett wondered if Rayna could understand what was being said. She moved behind him, his shirt clutched in her fist. He could smell her tears, taste her fear on the back of his tongue, thick and sweet. His beast roared at her distress and he followed with a growl that vibrated in his chest. The bones in his face started to shift and he clenched his teeth to hold the wolf back. When he spoke, his voice was harsh and rough. "You can't have her. She's mine!"

Caleb laughed, the sound grating and coarse. He stood, rising to his full height and stared down at him. "I don't smell a claim on her, Garrett. Crawl back to that pathetic life you've made for yourself and leave pack business to the real wolves. You're not wanted here." He lowered his voice and said, "You're only alive because some of us wish it."

It was then Carmen took a step forward. He would recognize her wolf anywhere. He locked gazes with her, watched as she lowered her head and growled. She snapped her teeth at him before taking a few steps to the side, her gaze locked on Rayna at his back.

Garrett glanced over at Malcolm. He was standing over Mitch, looking down at him. The man was still on the ground, blood pooling around his neck. The sight made him sick. Two seconds longer and that would have been Rayna.

Jacob was standing near them, a look of horror on his face. When he lifted his head and turned to look at him, Garrett tilted his head, gesturing for him to come and hoped the boy was still loyal to him. He knew the answer to that as he watched him edge his way to the tree line and disappear into the forest. He turned his attention back to Caleb and Carmen. "You'll have to come through me to get her, Caleb, and I can promise you, it'll be the last mistake you ever make."

The tone of his voice left no room for arguments. The soft whimpering of the others drew his gaze to them. They were watching him while backing away with ears and tails tucked in, their bodies low to the ground. The submissive behavior pleased his wolf. They were beta wolves and whether they knew it or not, they'd just submitted to him, telling him in actions he was stronger. They feared him. *Good. They should be.*

He looked back at Caleb. He wasn't backing down. His hair was bristled, standing on end with his ears erect. He met his gaze without fear.

A loud howl split the night air. It was Malcolm. The others turned and looked at him. Their leader was still standing in the middle of the circle. His plan was falling apart in front of him and he knew it. It showed on his face. When the others turned back to him, some started advancing, still trying to keep their distance, and circled around to the side.

Garrett lifted his head, looking at Malcolm. "I'll destroy them all, old man. Call them off!" Malcolm didn't answer. He just stood there staring at him but Garrett could see the uncertainty of the situation cross his face.

Sensing movement to his left, he glanced to the forest and saw Jacob. He stepped into the light and stopped beside him. "You know them better than I do, Jacob. Will they attack on Malcolm's order?"

"Caleb will regardless," he said, quietly. "He's always spoiling for a fight but the others I'm not so sure about. They fear you but they don't want to displease Malcolm either. Depends on who they fear more. You or Malcolm."

Garrett locked gazes with Caleb. He could see excitement flare in his eyes. Jacob was right. He was spoiling for a fight. "Can you outrun the others?"

"If I have to."

"You do," he said, pulling Rayna from behind him and placing her hand in Jacob's. "Take her to the hill where I found you. I'll come when I can."

"What are you going to do?"

Garrett straightened to his full height and inhaled deeply. He smiled and called his beast. "I'm going to show these puppies what a pissed off Alpha male looks like." He lunged for Caleb mid-shift. He didn't wait to see if Jacob had taken Rayna.

The impact with Caleb rolled them both. He was the first to his feet. As the last bone shifted, he straightened and looked at the others. They were circling him.

Without looking behind him he said, "Malcolm, if you want your pack to live, call them off. It doesn't have to end like this."

"I need her, Garrett. We'll do what we must."

"Then so will I." With teeth bared and claws extended, he howled, the sound echoing through the trees before he lowered his gaze on the wolves looking back at him and attacked.

"Slow down," Rayna said, panting for breath. Jacob had her by one hand and was dragging her through the forest. She couldn't see anything but the blur of trees as they ran.

The fear she'd felt back at the clearing was nothing compared to her fear for Garrett. What the hell was he even doing here! The fact they'd left him there, that Jacob had grabbed her and ran, leaving him to face those… creatures, alone, caused her already nervous stomach to heave.

"We can't slow down," Jacob yelled over his shoulder. "They're coming."

The minute the words were out of his mouth, Rayna heard them. The loud yelps and howls, the rustle and snapping of branches and the heavy footfalls of running. Her eyes widened and she quickened her steps, running at full speed.

She jerked her hand free from Jacob's grasp, pumping her fists at her sides and barreled through the trees. Jacob slowed until she passed him and put himself at her back.

"Take a straight path," he yelled. "The river isn't far ahead. We can lose them there."

The Calling

Panting, she ran. Ran like her life depended on it and judging the noise coming from behind her, it did. When the trees opened and revealed a grassy field, she slowed.

"Don't stop," Jacob said. "Come on. It's just a little further."

Her heart felt ready to burst as he grabbed her arm and kept running. Muscles she wasn't aware she had burned and ached. Her head throbbed, the blood pulsing through her veins rushed past her ears and each beat of her heart was felt as it vibrated in her body.

The sound of rushing water gave way to the smell of wet earth. She saw it then, the river, glistening in the moonlight.

They jumped in without pausing and swam to the other side.

When they reached the far bank, Jacob stopped and turned to her. "Go under," he said, a moment before putting a hand on her head and dunking her beneath the waters surface.

She sputtered and coughed when he let her up. "What the hell are you doing," she yelled.

"Trying to mask your scent." Dragging her to the bank, he reached down, scooping up a large handful of mud and rubbed it on her arms. "Cover what you can."

Rayna hesitated until he started covering his own body with the mud. She looked back over her shoulder at the opposite side of the river and froze. Dozens of wolves stood by the bank, watching them. "Jacob…"

He turned and looked before grabbing handfuls of mud and splattering her with it. "They won't cross the river," he said. "But hurry. They'll find a way across eventually."

She did as he asked, smearing the mud onto her body as fast as she could. A bitter laugh escaped her as she rubbed mud onto her clothes. When exactly had her life turned into a horror movie? She was being chased through the darkened woods by creatures that weren't supposed to exist. Werewolves! Honest to God, shape-shifting humans. It was too fantastic to believe. Too damn scary not to believe. When they both looked like they'd rolled in it, Jacob looked up at her.

"The hair too," he said.

Her eyes widened. "I have to rub that gunk in my hair?"

He smiled. "I can still smell your perfume. Jasmine, right? The others will smell it too. Cover everything."

She groaned and bent at the waist, scooping up more of the nasty, wet slick mud and coated her hair with it. It hung in wet clumps over her shoulders. When she was covered head to toe, Jacob grinned and grabbed her hand, pulling her from the riverbank and into the forest.

"Where are we going?"

"There's an old abandoned cabin not far from here. No one knows its there. You can barely see it for the overgrowth."

She followed him quietly for what seemed like miles. When the old cabin came into view, she stopped. "I'm not going in there."

Jacob turned to her, tilting his head to one side. "Why not?"

The Calling

She laughed. "For one thing the roof is sagging. What's to keep it from falling on our heads?"

"It won't. It's sturdier than it looks." He turned and crossed to the door. It scraped the floor as he opened it. When he vanished into the dark interior she huffed out a breath and followed.

"It's dark," he said. "But it'll keep us hidden. I can leave the door open. The light from the moon will brighten it enough for you to see."

"Thanks," she said, walking in and looking around the room. It was barren. Nothing but four walls and a crumbling fireplace. She walked around the small space, feeling the tiny jolts her muscles released as they tried to cool. She was out of breath and would have killed for a drop of water. Finally turning, she watched Jacob edge closer to the door and stare out. "How long do we have to stay here?"

"Just until Garrett comes."

Garrett. Regardless of how hateful he had been to her over the last eight months, Rayna had never been so happy to see him. Her heart had nearly stopped when she saw him dart from the trees. When he grabbed her and lifted her off her feet, placing her behind him and away from the others, she'd sobbed in relief. She'd clung to him and hadn't cared how he'd treated her in the past. Her fear of what was happening prevented any thought other than protecting herself. Luckily for her, she hadn't needed to. He'd done that for her. What he was even *doing here* was another question all together. He'd talked to Jacob like he knew him and that thought gave her pause. She looked back over at the boy. "How do you know him?" she asked. "Garrett, I mean."

Jacob shrugged. "He used to live here."

"He did?" *Garrett lived in a community of werewolves?*

"Yeah," Jacob said. "Before he moved to the city."

Rayna stared at him with a score of questions racing through her mind. "Why?" she said.

"Why what?"

"Why did he live here? I mean, why would he live in a town full of werewolves?"

"Why wouldn't he?"

She gaped at him and raised an eyebrow. "Because it's populated with werewolves, maybe?"

Jacob laughed. "Maybe because he is one."

Rayna's heart skipped a beat moments before her entire body went cold. She heard the words whisper through her head until she couldn't hear anything else. Her throat grew tight at the thought of Garrett turning into one of those… things. She took a deep breath, letting it out slowly before saying, "Garrett's a…" She couldn't even say it. She stared at Jacob and held her breath, waiting for him to say what she couldn't.

"A werewolf? You didn't know?" He glanced over his shoulder at her. "We all are. Everyone in Wolf's Creek is a shifter."

Her body went numb as her pulse started racing out of control. Visions of the wolves flashed before her minds eye. The horrifying shift she'd witnessed, wolf amber eyes that seemed to penetrate and devour, the razor sharp teeth, snarls and yelps, unearthly screams, howls and growls. Garrett was one of those… things? Her Garrett? The man she'd spent months giving herself to? She felt sick all of a sudden and sat down, putting her head between her knees. *Garret is a werewolf?* She almost laughed. It was absurd! How…? No. It wasn't possible. She'd spent six months with him. Six months with him in her life… in her bed. If he'd been one of those… No. Jacob was wrong. She would have known.

How would you have known? Did Bryce look anything less than human? Does Judith? Jacob?

No.

Garrett is a werewolf? Tears burnt her eyes and she stared at the dark floor between her feet and let them fall. Is that why he'd stopped seeing her? She raised her head and wiped her face. "How long?" she asked.

"How long what?"

"How long has Garrett been…"

He turned to look at her. "That's not my story to tell."

"How long?" she said again, almost growling the words.

He sighed and looked back out the door. "Twenty-six years."

Rayna gaped at him, stunned. "Twenty-six years?" she said, before running the numbers in her head. Her eyes widened. "He's been a werewolf since he was ten!"

Jacob laughed and turned to face her. "No. He was infected when he was twenty-four."

Now she was completely confused.

"We don't age like humans, remember?" Jacob said. "The aging process slows down. Its why we remain hidden."

"Twenty-six years?" She did the math inside her head again and laughed. "So, you're telling me that Garret is—"

"Close to fifty?" he said, grinning. "Give or take a few years. I can't remember his exact age but that's probably pretty damn close."

Rayna laughed louder and the tears were back. She blinked them away and shook her head. "You're crazy," she said. "You're all crazy." She stood and paced the length of the cabin, the entire night replaying inside her head. She still couldn't believe half of it but she'd seen it with her own eyes. Werewolves really existed. They shifted shape under a full moon and were ten times scarier than any movie she'd ever seen. Monsters were real and Garrett was one of them. Her chest hurt with that bit of knowledge. Garrett was one of those... monsters. The reality of it was mind numbing. The attack she'd witnessed was even scarier. The moment she thought of it, and of Mitch, tears bit at the back of her eyes. Looking up she asked, "Did they kill him?"

"Who?" Jacob asked.

"Mitch."

He shook his head. "No. He was still breathing when I saw him. I don't think their intention was to kill him. You either for that matter."

"Did you know?"

"Know what?"

"What Malcolm had planned?"

"No."

She wasn't sure she believed him but something in his eyes told her she could trust him. When he turned and slid down the wall by the door and sat down, he leaned his head back and looked at her.

"I don't agree with Malcolm's method but what he's trying to do is for the benefit of us all."

The Calling

"And what exactly does he hope to accomplish?"

"The majority of us just want to live normal lives," he said. "To be able to do normal things. Go to McDonalds for a hamburger or go to the movies. We don't have any of that here. We have to travel over thirty miles just for the supplies we need. There's nothing here."

"What about the town?"

He grinned. "It's just for show in case anyone stumbles on us. There's nothing there, not really."

"Then why bother erecting buildings if nothing is there?"

"We didn't. The town was abandoned when the old ones found it. They pooled their resources and bought the land. Most of the mountain is owned by the pack. No one bothers us here and we don't venture out unless we have to."

"Why not," she asked, stopping by the crumbling fireplace. "Other than the whole shifting thing, you all look perfectly normal. You can blend in as well as I do." Garrett did, she added silently to herself.

"We still have to shift once a month, regardless of where we are. Imagine living next door to one of us. How do you think the average person will handle that if they ever found out? If people knew we existed, they would be more likely to shoot first and ask questions later."

He shrugged his shoulders and looked back out the door. "A rogue wolf is what got most of the pack into this mess. In Atlanta, thirty years ago. He, the wolf, was living outside the city and someone saw him when he shifted. When they came after him, he snapped. He went on a killing spree and infected most of everyone you saw here. Those that didn't die immediately were quarantined. When the first one shifted, they killed him and locked the others up. When they started experimenting on them, Malcolm is the one who got them all out."

"So you think that would happen again?"

"Malcolm thinks so. If word got out about what we were, we'd be hunted down and killed on sight. If people knew about us, and accepted us, then we'd have a chance. Thirty years is a long time to live in fear of being found. The men who initially captured Malcolm and the others know we exist. I'm surprised we haven't been found yet. I'm sure it's only a matter of time though. It's why we live so isolated up here on the mountain."

"Well, what about you," she said. "You haven't been here as long as the others. You're not old enough. You're just a child."

His eyes burned fierce the minute the words were out of her mouth and his cheeks turned red. "I'm twenty-six years old."

Rayna's eyes widened. "You're twenty-six?"

"I told you we don't age as humans do and I'm not a child." He got to his feet and looked back out the door.

"I'm sorry," Rayna said. "I didn't mean to offend you."

He shrugged a shoulder but didn't say anything for long minutes. "I don't have any family," he said. "I was living in the next town over the first time I realized there were others like me. I scented them when they were getting supplies and followed them back. Found this place," he said, looking through the cabin, "and this is where Garrett found me. He took me in and gave me his place when he left."

"Were you born a shifter?"

"No. I was attacked right after my sixteenth birthday. No one is born a werewolf. You have to be made into one."

"How?"

"A bite most of the time. A scratch if it's deep enough."

She remembered the scar on Garrett's side. The wide, deep scar that started just below his ribcage and ended at his hip. He'd told her it was from a dog attack when he was a child. Now she had to wonder if that wasn't how he'd ended up one of those things. A chill ran up her spine just thinking about it. She focused her eyes on Jacob and said, "And you? How did you end up a werewolf?"

He turned his head and grabbed the back of his shirt, lifting it up and turning toward the filtered light coming from the door. Rayna gasped when she saw the scars. Deep, white lines ran from his left shoulder down the length of his back. They were wide, the claw marks still visible. "How long ago did that happen?"

"Ten years ago give or take a few months."

Jacob looked up suddenly and in a blur of movement, darted from the door, ducking behind the wall before turning his head to her. He held a finger to his lips, motioning for her to stay quiet. Peeking around the corner, he looked out, scanning the area before looking back at her.

His eyes had bled to amber.

"Stay here. Do not leave under any circumstances."

Rayna froze. "Don't you dare leave me here," she whispered.

"I won't go far. Something's out there. I need room to shift in case its one of the others."

He left without another word and Rayna stared at the empty doorway. She couldn't see anything beyond the rotted planks on the porch and backed up until she hit the wall. Seconds turned to long minutes. When Jacob didn't return the fear worked its way back up her spine. She edged her way to the door, peeking out into the darkness. Nothing moved. Not even the trees. It was completely still.

When her heart started pounding, she grabbed the edge of the door. The desire to run outside and find the only person halfway possible of saving her was strong, but she knew better. But what if Jacob didn't come back or wasn't able to? What if the others found her? A glance around the cabin showed her what she already knew. There wasn't anywhere to hide.

The sound of rustling bushes caught her attention and Rayna turned back to the door, her worst fear realized when she saw a wolf standing in front of the cabin.

She jumped back and screamed, her lungs aching from the strain. The wolf stepped up on the porch and walked through the door toward her. She stumbled and fell, hitting her head on something that caused her ears to ring and bright flashes of light to burst in front of her eyes.

The last thing she saw was the wolf reaching for her.

Six

"What the hell did you do?"

Garrett turned to the door and growled, crouching low over Rayna's body. When he saw it was Jacob, he straightened and said, "I didn't do anything. She saw me and freaked."

"I wonder why?" Jacob said, raising a brow at him. "Did you bleed every wolf you came in contact with?"

"Not nearly enough of them."

Jacob grinned and walked across the room. "Is she all right?"

"I don't know. I don't want to touch her."

"Why?"

Garrett held up hands that barely looked human. They were covered in blood with bits of fur and flesh under his claws.

Jacob grimaced when he looked. "Good idea," he said. He knelt beside Rayna and grabbed her shoulder, giving her a light shake. "Rayna? It's Jacob. Can you hear me?"

She didn't move. Jacob shook her a few more times before moving her head. "Damn," he said. "That's going to leave a knot." A broken rock from the fireplace was under her head. She wasn't bleeding but Garrett knew she'd have a hell of a headache when she woke up.

"I think she'll be okay," Jacob said. "Probably just knocked herself out."

Garrett nodded. He stared down at her, noticing the mud covering her body. A quick glance at Jacob and he grunted. "Came across the river?"

"Yes. How'd you know?"

"The mud."

"Oh." Jacob tossed the rock away before giving her shoulder another light shake. "Rayna, it's Jacob. Come on now, wake up."

Jacob looked up and raked a gaze over him, sniffing the air. "Can you shift back? It's probably not a good idea to look like that when she wakes up."

Garrett looked down at himself and nodded. "Probably, but her waking up and seeing me butt-ass naked and still covered in blood won't help either. Besides, if they find us, I won't be able to shift back."

Jacob sighed. "Fine," he said, "but I wouldn't be hovering over her when she wakes up. She's not handling any of this too well, especially the furry-you parts."

That's what he'd been afraid of since the day he met her. Her reaction to him when she found out what he was. Garrett stared down at her for long moments before walking to the far side of the cabin, trying to stick to the shadows. He didn't want to scare her anymore than she already was. He could still taste her fear on the back of his tongue. It was probably the only thing that kept him fighting the pack so viciously instead of doing the smart thing and fleeing when he realized he was outnumbered. Of course, he'd never backed down from a fight and for the first time ever, he actually had a reason to fight. They'd threatened his chosen mate. Tried to hurt her and scared her half to death. For that fact alone they all deserved to bleed.

He'd torn into the pack without a care for his own safety. He saw red by the time the last one fell. The others, the ones who knew they were no match for him, left as soon as he attacked. The Alphas who thought they were strong enough to take him found out quickly how wrong they were. Caleb had gotten away but not unscathed. He left a trail Garrett been tempted to follow but making sure Rayna was safe, and that none of the others had reached her, prevented him from even looking.

He heard Rayna make a small sound in the back of her throat moments later. Her head moved to one side and he saw Jacob lean down over her.

"That's it. Open your eyes," Jacob said.

Her body jolted all of a sudden and she gasped. Jacob grabbed her shoulders and said, "It's okay. You're safe."

She pushed his hands away and sat up, wincing before looking at the door. "I saw a wolf."

"Yeah. It was just Garrett."

"Garrett," she said, turning her head quickly and scanning the room. She looked past him, only to glance back a moment later. He knew the instant she saw him. Her body stiffened and her eyes widened.

He locked gazes with her and she held it, unmoving. The hair on his back bristled and he scented her on the air. The soft fragrance of flowers was faint, masked by mud, but it was still there. Fresh, clean. His Rayna. It affected him the same as it always did. Caused his body to ache. Covered head to toe in mud and he still wanted her. He inhaled again, savoring the delicate scent of her but smelled fear this time. It overpowered everything else. He realized then her fear was of him.

"Can you stand?" Jacob asked her.

She nodded before finally climbing to her feet with Jacob's help. When she continued to stare at him, Garrett leaned back into the shadows.

Rayna was torn between running like a frightened cat and crossing the room to get a better look at Garrett. He was trying, not too successfully, to hide in a darkened corner. Her heart was racing as she stared at him. He stood well over six and a half foot tall, the hair covering his body washed away by the inky blackness engulfing the darkened cabin. His eyes were the same as the others' had been. Glowing, wolf amber. They looked like two pinpricks in the dark. He was impossibly big, scary even from across the room, and her heart ached as she stared at him. How had he kept this secret from her for so long? How could she not know?

Seeing Jacob out of the corner of her eye she glanced over at him. His eyes seemed to glow out of his mud-covered face. Seeing him reminded her of her own muddy state. She raised a hand, feeling her stiff chunks of hair and cringed, darting a glance to the corner. In all the time she'd known Garrett the worst he'd ever seen her look was when she crawled out of bed with her hair a mess and no make-up on. She could barely see him now.

The Calling

If it weren't for the eerie glow of his eyes, he'd be lost in the shadows, but she had no doubt he could see her. Tearing her eyes away from him she leaned toward Jacob and whispered, "He's here now. Can we go? We need to find Mitch and I want to shower." As vain as it was, she didn't want Garrett to see her looking so shabby.

Jacob smiled. "There's no need to whisper," he said, whispering back. "He can hear you regardless."

She blushed. The heat burned hot on her cheeks and down her neck. She straightened and looked at anything other than the corner where Garrett stood. When he moved and started across the room, the soft clicking tap of his clawed feet hitting the wooden floor echoed in the stillness.

"She's right," Garrett said. "We can't stay here."

Rayna did look up then. Garrett's voice was rough, tinged with a rasping gargle that sounded otherworldly. It was much deeper in tone than his normal speaking voice and no matter how hard she tried, she couldn't help *but* stare. As he neared her, she took an involuntary step back.

He stopped and looked at her. "I'm not going to hurt you, Rayna."

The voice sounded different and the eyes looking down at her weren't familiar, but she knew as she looked up at him that he wouldn't. He might be an ass, and cut her with his barbed comments, but she knew he wouldn't' physically hurt her. If he had wanted to do that, he'd had plenty of chances in the past.

"We can't take her back to the main house," Jacob said. "They'll be waiting on her."

"I know."

"Any suggestions?"

Garrett looked at her and said, "Yeah. My truck is parked out by the creek, near the ridge. Get her to it and hit the highway. Don't stop until the sun comes up."

Rayna's eyes widened. "No!" she said. "I can't leave Mitch here."

"He's fine."

"I'll see that for myself first," she said.

"Did you see what they did with him?" Jacob asked. "Was he still alive?"

"He was. They took him not long after the fight started."

"We've got to go get him," Rayna said, looking from Garrett to Jacob. "I can't leave him here."

"I'll make sure your boyfriend makes it back home, Rayna."

She shot him a cold look. "He's not my boyfriend, Garrett, and you know it."

He made a sound deep in his throat. Not exactly a growl but… something. She stared at him and even though he looked nothing like the man she knew, the way he was carrying himself now reminded her of him. You can't disguise that much arrogance no matter how much fang and fur you threw over it.

"We'll get him," Jacob said. "But first, we've got to get you out of here."

"I'm not leaving," she said, defiantly, crossing her arms under her breast. "Not until I see for myself that Mitch is fine."

"This isn't the time for your stubbornness, Rayna."

"And I have no desire to take orders from you, Garrett."

He did growl that time and the sound rattled her bones. It also caused goose bumps to pimple her skin and made the hair on the back of her neck stand up. He took a step toward her and it took every ounce of courage she possessed to not take a step back. Lord knew she was ready to piss herself having him so close to her looking the way he did.

Jacob stepped in between them and said, "Let's just find a safe place to hideout at the moment. You two can fight when we're in the clear." He looked up at Garrett and smiled. "Do you think they would suspect your old place?"

Garrett's eyes narrowed slightly before his chest expanded. He didn't say anything for long minutes, just stood there staring at Jacob.

When he turned and started for the door, Rayna exhaled the breath she'd been holding and watched him cross the room. He was huge. The light shining through the door showed the hair on his body to be a deep, dark, midnight black. His shoulders took up most of the doorway and he appeared even taller against the height of the doorframe. He stopped and ducked under the doorway, stepping out onto the porch and looking back over his shoulder. His gaze found hers and held. "Take her. Follow the river. I'll be there when I can."

He was gone in a blur of movement. Rayna stared at the spot he'd been standing, thoughts of talking wolves and humans for dinner running through her mind. When Jacob touched her arm and motioned for the door, she followed without a word.

Rayna tucked the end of her towel into place and lifted her hand, wiping the steam from the mirror over the sink. She was scrubbed clean and she felt almost normal.

The trek through the woods had been worse than their mad dash from the pack. They'd walked for what seemed like miles through the thick, overgrown forest. She'd stumbled on logs and got tangled in a patch of briars that bit into her skin and drew tiny pricks of blood to the surface of her skin. By the time they reached Jacob's cabin, Garrett's old cabin, she'd been ready to fall down and sleep right where she landed.

She was exhausted, mentally and physically, but knew sleep wouldn't come anytime soon. The images playing inside her head wouldn't let her.

Dropping the towel, she finished drying and grabbed the clothes Jacob had given her. A dark blue t-shirt and a pair of boxer shorts, which he'd found in Garrett's overnight bag laying on the front porch. The clothes smelled like Garrett and she held them to her face and inhaled his scent. Her eyes closed, his image flashing in her mind's eye and for the second time that night, tears burned behind her eyelids when she thought of him and what he was.

She sniffed the tears back and slipped the clothes on, rolling the waist of the shorts down to keep them from falling and looked back at the mirror. Her clothes had been thrown in the wash, along with her underwear and she wished now she had her bra. Walking into the other room with her nipples shining through the thin shirt wasn't on her to do list, especially when a teenage boy was sitting in there. She shook her head and laughed. If Jacob had been telling her the truth earlier, a teen was something he wasn't. He was twenty-six.

And Garrett was fifty, not thirty-five like he'd told her.

She shook the thought away and looked around the small bathroom. A robe hung on the back of the door and she grabbed it, slipping it on, before tying the belt.

Opening the door, she made her way down the short hall back to the living room. Jacob was standing by the window looking out. Her pulse quickened instantly. "Have they found us?"

He turned to look at her and shook his head. "No, but they will eventually."

Her eyes widened at the admission. "Then why did you suggest we come here?"

"Because we didn't have any other choice and this will be the last place they'll think to look. Knowing Caleb, he'll think we're halfway down the mountain, not hiding under their nose." He stared at her for long minutes before sighing. "Once Garrett gets back, we'll figure out what to do."

"Garrett left before us," she said. "Why isn't he here already?"

He looked as if he didn't want to answer before he seemed to shrug his whole body and said, "He had to feed. Shifting takes a lot of energy. Shifting back to human form takes more. Besides, I'd bet my tail he's over at

Malcolm's seeing what they're up to. If there was any immediate danger, he'd be here."

He walked across the room and stopped when he reached the hall. "I need to shower. The kitchen is stocked. Help yourself to whatever you like." And with that, he disappeared down the hall to the bathroom, leaving her alone for the first time all day.

Rayna wrapped her arms around herself and took in her surroundings. Jacob had said this place belonged to Garrett at one time. It was nothing compared to the apartment he had back in Bluff's Point. It was hardly a shack but everything was so dark. There were only three windows in the living room. The sofas and chairs were covered in dark blue fabric. Two bookshelves sat on the wall opposite the front door, their shelves stuffed with broken spine books and magazines. A television sat between them and a recliner with a small table and lamp sat in the corner. It was rustic and one glance at the room told you a man lived here. There wasn't a frill anywhere.

The kitchen was small but clean, with a table with four chairs around it. Her stomach growled the instant she looked at the refrigerator and she realized then she hadn't eaten since noon.

She felt odd snooping but crossed the room to the kitchen anyway. Opening the refrigerator door, she looked at the contents inside before grabbing a bottle of water, twisting off the cap, and drinking half of it before stopping.

Leftovers and lunchmeat for sandwiches was all the refrigerator offered. As hungry as she was, nothing held any appeal. She shut the door and walked back to the living room, sitting on the sofa and sipped her water.

The Calling

The day replayed in her mind again and she still had a hard time believing it. Werewolves were real and Garrett was one of them. Her heart felt heavy with the knowledge. She'd spent months with him, even entertaining the thoughts of spending the rest of her life with him and then... he'd dumped her. Tossed her away as if she meant nothing to him.

Why had things gone so wrong? First Garrett and then Malcolm. Just thinking of Malcolm caused her stomach to sour. How could she have been so gullible? Malcolm had been begging her for the past six months to visit his town. That alone should have thrown up warning flags but she let her boss, and Mitch, bully her into doing something she really had no desire to do. From now on, she'd trust her gut instinct.

She wished she had done it earlier, back at the house. Her luggage was still there and waiting in a hidden pocket was a bit of protection she wished she had at the moment. Werewolves or not, unless they could move faster than a speeding bullet, she had all she needed to find Mitch and get them out of town.

Sitting her water on the table by the sofa, she sank down into the cushions, curling into the corner and covering her legs with the end of the robe. Her mind was awash with images that she knew would give her nightmares for months to come, the biggest one was the knowledge that Garrett was one of the monsters.

"Does he still live?"

"Yes."

Malcolm sighed in relief and sat down. "Watch him closely. With Ms. Ford gone, he's our only hope of getting her back. We've worked too hard to let this plan fall to pieces now. The others won't be pleased if we fail."

"We'll find her. Caleb is the best tracker we have."

"I know, but Caleb isn't in any shape to look for her at the moment and Garrett will more than likely move her as quickly as possible. They could be half way across the state by now."

"No one is looking? Why not?"

"Have you seen them, Stan? Any of them?"

"No. Are there many injured?"

Malcolm laughed bitterly. "We have two dead and over a dozen injured. Garrett tore through them like they were pups. Imagine what he could do if he had time to plan an attack." He stilled and shook his head. "How did this get so out of control? It was a simple plan. Why didn't it work?"

Stan sat down in the chair opposite Malcolm and sighed. "Garrett Kincaid is why," he said. "We should have taken more precautions and picked someone else the moment we found out those two were involved."

"But they weren't involved. The scouts said they'd parted ways."

"So he said. We don't know anything other than what was seen."

Malcolm scowled and leaned back in his chair. "This is a complication we don't need. Garrett was strong when he left twelve years ago. The way he tore through this pack makes me wonder if he couldn't overthrow me if he had the desire to do so."

"He won't."

"We can't be sure of that," Malcolm said.

"He wants the girl. Maybe we should just let him have her," Stan said.

"We can't do this without the girl, Stan. It has to be her. If we start over, it will put us months behind. I can't go through all this again."

"Well, Garrett isn't going to just let us have her. He was always bull-headed. He never followed pack dictates like the others did. If he's as strong as you say, he could single-handedly destroy us all."

"Yes, but if we can get her back, it will be too late for him to do anything. Once we infect her, he'll have no choice but to do as we want."

"And what of the others?"

Malcolm looked around the room as Stan's softly spoken words reached him. They were alone but he wasn't naïve enough to think no one was listening. "They're being watched. If I find proof of their deceit, I'll make an example out of them all."

"So what should we do?" Stan asked.

Malcolm stared at the floor, his shoulders sagging. "We have to get Ms. Ford back but we must care for our dead first. In all the time we've been here, we've never had a death born of such violence. The pack will expect us to do something. Finding Ms. Ford isn't going to be their main concern at the moment, but call the wolves. See how many are willing to face Garrett again. We'll need strength in numbers, so we may have to force them.

We have to get Ms. Ford back before the others arrive. This entire plan hinges on her."

"And Garrett?"

Malcolm stared at his most trusted friend and knew what he was thinking. He could see it in his eyes. He nodded his head and said, "We'll kill him if we have to."

Carmen moved away from the door and walked to the stairs, climbing them carefully as to not alert Malcolm she was there. When she reached the top, she ignored the looks the others gave her and walked the length of the hall before entering the last room on the left without a word. Mitch was on the bed, his body trembling as sweat soaked the sheets under him. She smiled and moved further into the room. "He'll live?"

"Of course."

She sat on the edge of the bed, running a finger down the side of Mitch's face. "Malcolm suspects something."

"And I wonder why that is?" he said, glaring at her. "I think he's on to us. You should have never called Garrett."

Her eyes bled to amber as she looked up. "Garrett's participation is pivotal to our plan or have you forgotten? Without him we have nothing."

"I don't know why you think we can't do this on our own."

The Calling

"Because you aren't strong enough to take Malcolm yourself, that's why."

"Is that the only reason?" She answered him with a smile. He scowled and walked around the bed. "If I didn't know any better, Carmen, I'd think you had plans of keeping Garrett for yourself."

"You worry too much, lover. My desire for Garrett is only to get us what we want. Nothing more."

"And why don't I believe you?"

She grinned as she stood to face him. "Trust me. Once Garrett kills Malcolm, you and I will be in complete control of the pack, just like we planned. Garrett can take his newly turned bitch and go about his life."

He stared at her, the look on his face showing her his doubt. She reached out, running her fingers up his thigh before cupping him through his jeans. He grew hard in her hand. "I promise you," she said, leaning up to kiss him, "all will go as planned. Bring me the girl, and Garrett, and we'll spend the rest of our lives with you as king."

Seven

Rayna jolted awake and stared wide-eyed around the room. It was still dark, the only light coming from the open curtains on the windows that let the glow of the moon filter in. She sat up, looked around again trying to see what had woken her. She didn't see anyone or hear anything. She sighed and pushed her hair out of her face before working a hand through the tangled ends. It had dried in wild strands that took a few minutes of finger combing to straighten out.

Standing, she stretched and walked to the window, looking out. The moon was still bright, illuminating the surrounding forest. A glance at her watch showed it to be a little after one a.m.

Thoughts of Mitch had plagued her dreams. The sound of his screams echoed in her head and the blood that poured from his neck still made her stomach queasy. She wondered how he was, if he was still alive. She felt responsible even though he'd been the one who wanted to make this trip. Malcolm's plan, from what she'd gathered, was meant for her. Mitch just happened to be in the wrong place at the wrong time.

Crossing her arms under her breasts, she laid her head against the windowpane and stared at nothing. They'd be coming for her. Jacob even said as much. What would they do with her when they did? Did her fate match that of Mitch's? Would they attack her and tear at her flesh the way they had him? She shuddered at the thought. No. Garrett wouldn't let them. Regardless of how much he hated her, she knew he wouldn't let anyone hurt her. He'd proved that already.

Hearing a noise behind her, she turned her head to the sound. Garrett walked into the room and crossed to the kitchen. All she could do was stare at him.

He looked… normal. He'd shed the wolf guise and was freshly showered, judging his attire. He wore nothing but a white towel draped low on his hips. He opened the refrigerator door, grabbing a bottle of water before turning. He froze when he saw her and stared for long moments before letting the refrigerator door shut.

Neither said anything. They just stood there looking at each other.

Rayna couldn't have spoken if she tried.

Staring at him, she tried to imagine the man she saw now as the… wolf she'd seen earlier. She couldn't. Nothing about this man gave her any indication of the creature he was. *I guess that's how he hid it for so long.*

She let her gaze roam over every inch of him, from his strong jaw line to the high cheekbones and pale brown eyes tinged with long lashes. His skin was still tanned and of the few men she'd ever been with, Garrett had to be the most fit. His biceps were impressive, as was the rest of him. His chest was solid, tight abs that dipped and curved and sharp hipbones that formed a perfect "V" and drew her eye to the top of the towel. The dark dusting of hair that peeked out from the top of it and ran up to his navel caused her breath to catch. He was so beautiful he caused her chest to ache. *Beautiful he may be, but he hates you, remember?*

The familiar ache returned to her chest and she turned her head, looking back out the window.

Garrett's pulse raced by the time Rayna looked away from him. She hadn't looked at him like that in longer than he cared to remember. His body tightened almost painfully and he wanted her gaze back on him, wanted to see her look at him as if she still wanted him.

Inhaling deeply, he scented her on the air. His wolf slid under his flesh like liquid through his veins when he caught the scent of her. The delicate aroma of flowers was gone, now… the heady musk of her arousal filled the air mixed with his own scent. She was wearing his clothes, his scent lingering on her skin. The wolf howled in his head and a growl worked it way up his chest, vibrating against his ribs and firing off every nerve in his body.

The wolf had wanted her from the moment he'd first laid eyes on her over a year ago. Now that she was in his old house, surrounded by the things he'd left to Jacob and wrapped in his scent, he knew the beast wouldn't rest until it possessed her. If he could just find a way to do it without infecting her, he would put himself out of misery and claim her.

She looked back over at him, the light from the window shining off her hair and throwing shimmers of copper and gold across the strands. She lifted a hand, pulling the edge of the robe she wore shut before pushing her hair away from her face.

He straightened, sat the water bottle in his hand on the counter and cleared his throat, forcing his beast down and trying to keep his voice soft. "It's probably not a good idea to stand next to the windows."

Her eyes widened before she glanced back out. "They're really going to come for me, aren't they?" She looked back over at him. "Jacob said they would."

"More than likely they will, and they could have you snatched out of that window before I could get to you."

Taking a few steps away from the window, she turned and put her back to the wall. She said nothing for long minutes, just stood there staring at him. When she finally spoke, her voice was quiet with a soft tremble. "I guess I owe you my gratitude," she said. "It's hard to tell what they would have done to me if you hadn't been there."

"You don't need to thank me, and I don't think their intention is to kill you, if that's what you're worried about."

"Maybe not, but the alternative doesn't sound too pleasant either."

He smiled and tilted his head to one side. "Being a wolf isn't all that bad," he said. "It has its advantages."

"So Malcolm said."

"He was right."

"How so?"

"Well, you can live longer than the average human for one."

"Being immortal isn't worth turning into a…" She cut her words off but he could tell by the look on her face what she was about to say. He was a monster in her eyes. Something vile and disgusting. His chest ached at the revelation and his face must have reflected his pain.

She ducked her head and said, "I'm sorry."

He forced a smile onto his face and shrugged one shoulder. "It's fine."

"No," she said, looking back up. "It's not. I should be thanking you for saving my life, not insulting you."

He looked her in the eye and said, "You don't have to thank me, Rayna… there isn't anything I wouldn't do for you."

She stared at him and he could tell she didn't believe him. And really, why should she? When was the last time he had a kind word for her? The day he left her standing in the middle of the park crying? No. That was the day he told her he'd just used her and thanked her for the best piece of ass he'd ever had. Maybe the day before that, when he tried to tell her they were over but ended up fucking her silly instead. No, not that day either. He couldn't even remember and he hated himself just a little bit more because of it.

He sighed and ran a hand through his hair. "Look, I know I've been a complete ass to you for months now and you don't have to forgive me… ever really, but I want you to know it wasn't personal."

"You hating me isn't personal?" She laughed softly and looked away from him, staring down at the floor.

"I don't hate you, Rayna."

"Could have fooled me."

She whispered so softly that without his keen hearing he would have never heard it. "I don't hate you."

She looked back up, her eyes glistening with unshed tears. "Then why?"

The Calling

Because I love you and I wanted you safe. Because I never wanted you to know what I am. He swallowed the words before he voiced them.

"Is it because..." she paused, her eyes becoming brighter with tears. "Because of what you are... or was it just me?"

Her voice trembled and he gritted his teeth together to keep from baring his soul. Being in the same room with her, alone, with no one to see how he acted around her left him defenseless. It was easy to pretend when they were in the real world, surrounded by people, but not here. Not now. Not after everything that had happened tonight. He came too close to losing her. He still could and that little piece of knowledge terrified the hell out of him.

He crossed the room, stopping when he reached her. "It wasn't you," he said, softly. "I never wanted to hurt you. It damn near killed me every time I did." Her bottom lip trembled as she stared at him and the look on her face nearly did him in. Hurting her with words he didn't mean scorched him to the bone, seeing the effects of those words nearly ripped out his soul. He sighed when a tear fell down her cheek. He raised his hand and brushed it away with his thumb, staring down at her. "I'm sorry, Rayna. For everything."

One tear turned into two and before he could catch them, the dam broke. He grabbed her, pulling her to him and buried his face in her hair as she cried. She felt so good, smelled so good, he wrapped his arms around her tighter, nearly sighing in relief when he felt her arms circle his waist.

Her tears intensified, her breath hot against his bare chest. He rubbed his face into her hair, his fingers climbing into the thick strands before he kissed the top of her head. He lingered there, holding her tighter before she lifted her head and looked up at him. He wiped her tears away, his fingers sliding easily across her wet face and the reasons he had for pushing her away vanished.

One look at her sweet, ripe mouth and his body responded immediately. His chest felt tight, his pulse raced just a little bit faster and the moment he saw her tongue slip between her lips to moisten them, he was done for. He leaned down and kissed her.

Her arms tightened around him immediately, her mouth opening under his as her tongue pushed inside his mouth. Months of wanting her and the need he denied himself tore at his flesh and the wolf howled triumphantly inside his head. He devoured her mouth, sucking on her tongue until she moaned and went soft and pliant in his arms. Her hands gripped his arms before sliding over his ribs, slim fingers tickling his chest and stomach and he hardened in an instant. He leaned into her, his knee parting her thighs and the desire to strip her bare and take her right there against the wall screamed through his head. He broke the kiss before he lost all reason to think. He stared down at her, his lungs heaving for air as she stared up at him. "If I could take it all back, I would. It drove me crazy to see you and not have you. The only way I even dared speak to you was to insult you." He cupped her face in his hands, kissed her again, his lips tasting and teasing her own. "I never wanted to hurt you, Rayna."

"Then why did you?" she asked.

The Calling

He shook his head before laying his forehead against hers and closing his eyes. "I didn't know any other way."

"Any other way to what?"

"Make you hate me." She didn't say anything but her arms tightened around his waist. "I knew I couldn't stay away from you so I hoped you'd solve the problem for me. If you hated me, you would avoid me."

"Why? Because you're different?"

"For the most part, yes," he said, leaning back to look at her. "I never wanted you to know, Rayna." He sighed and ran his fingers through her hair, brushing his lips across her face. Her warmth seeped into his bones and if he were able to purr, he was sure the wolf would be doing just that at the moment. He felt at peace for the first time in months. All because she was in his arms, her sweet breath on his face and her hands touching his bare flesh. How long she'd let him keep her there was a question he wasn't sure he wanted the answer to. After the way he'd treated her, she owed him nothing. "It's late," he said. "You should sleep. You'll need all the rest you can get."

She stared at him for long moments before finally nodding her head and let go of him. He reluctantly took a step back. "Take the bed. Last door on the left."

"Where will you be?"

"I'll take the couch." She gave him a look that he wanted to interpret as her wanting to disagree and as much as sharing a bed with her again caused the wolf to howl inside his head, he couldn't afford the distraction. "I need to be close to the door in case they try to come before daybreak."

She watched him for long minutes before nodding her head and starting across the room. She paused behind the sofa, looking back over her shoulder at him. "Good night."

"Good night, Rayna."

The smell of food and the clatter of dishes woke her. The sun was shining; bright rays peeked through the blinds on the window and Rayna squinted and rolled over, away from the light, and looked around the room.

It was tidy, much like the rest of the house, and she burrowed into the blankets, stealing what warmth was still there.

When she'd climbed underneath the blankets and closed her eyes the night before, her dreams hadn't been of monsters chasing her through darkened forests. They had been of Garrett. After months of his hurtful words and hateful glances, he'd kissed her. Kissed her like the world was ending and he couldn't get enough of her. Kissed her like he used to. Like she was the only thing that mattered to him. Like he wanted her… craved her. The feeling left her elated and confused.

Had he told her the truth when he said he'd broken things off with her not because of her, but because of what he was? That he'd tried to make her hate him because it was easier to stay away? How different things would have been if he'd just trusted her enough to be honest. *And what would you have done if he had? Screamed while running as fast as you could or just passed out?* She sighed.

The Calling

All of the above, probably, and he knew that. He'd done what he thought was best, regardless of how hurtful it had been.

She rolled over, staring up at the ceiling before lifting her arms and stretching. Sitting up, she pushed the blankets back and stood, slipped the robe she'd found the night before back on, and walked to the bedroom door.

Jacob was in the kitchen, singing something under his breath. He was placing a dish of something on the table and she smelled coffee and toast. Her stomach growled a moment later. She was starved.

Walking to the bathroom, she opened the door and came face to face with Garrett. "Oh! I'm sorry," she said.

He was standing in front of the mirror, wiping his face with a towel, a razor and a can of shaving cream on the sink in front of him. He looked over at her and smiled. "Good morning."

She took a step back and stopped when he spoke. "Good morning."

"I think our breakfast is almost ready. Jacob has been making enough noise to wake half the valley."

"I know. The clanking of dishes is what woke me."

He tossed the towel in his hand into the hamper by the tub and turned, walking toward her. He was dressed in jeans and a white t-shirt that hugged his chest. Although the sight of him practically naked was always nice, this was in no way a disappointment.

The man was still gorgeous, shape-shifting wolf or not.

She stared up at him when he stopped in front of her. He hadn't left but a breath of space between them and one deep inhale would be all it took to touch him. She was tempted, but wasn't sure of his intentions toward her. She wasn't going to presume anything. Just because he'd kissed her didn't mean he'd changed his mind and wanted her back. It could have been nothing more than the heat of the moment kind of thing. She wasn't about to make a fool out of herself by thinking it meant more.

His gaze roamed her face, stopping briefly on her lips before continuing down the line of her body. Her flesh tingled and the tightening she felt in her stomach whenever he looked at her returned with a vengeance. She swallowed to moisten her throat when he smiled at her.

"I could stand here all day looking at you," he said, "But our breakfast is getting cold."

"Yeah. Probably." The words came out sounding breathy even to her. She shifted on her feet and her back hit the doorframe. That's when she realized she was blocking the door. "Oh!" she said, feeling her cheeks heat up when his smile widened. "Sorry." She moved to the side, giving him room to pass. He continued to look at her for long moments before he leaned down and placed a soft kiss on her cheek. He leaned back, raising his hand and brushed his thumb across her jaw before finally smiling and walking past her. The second he was out of sight, she let out the breath she'd been holding and grabbed the door, shutting it with a soft click.

The Calling

"Any clue what we should do?" Jacob asked.

"Yeah. Get Rayna as far from Wolf's Creek as possible." Garrett leaned back against the cabinet and crossed his arms over his chest. He stared down the hall, watching for her. When she didn't appear he turned to Jacob. "Are the others going along with this plan Malcolm has? To infect Rayna and have her expose the wolves to the public?"

"As far as I can tell they are."

"And no one has a problem with it?" Jacob shrugged his shoulders and looked away. Garrett narrowed his eyes and tilted his head to one side. "Did you know about this, Jacob?"

"No!" he said, looking back up at him. "I swear, man. I mean, I knew Malcolm was trying to get a reporter here to tell our story but that was it. I didn't know he wanted to infect her. You know they don't tell me shit."

"But the others knew?"

"Most of them, I guess. Come on, Garrett. You know how they are. They'd jump in front of a moving bus if Malcolm told them to do it. They think he's God."

Garrett's temper flared suddenly at the thought of Malcolm, and the others, luring Rayna here with the intentions of harming her. Harming *his* woman. "Well, their *God*, just caused them a shit load of problems." He pushed away from the cabinet and grabbed the plates, laying them out on the table and tried to get his temper under control. He felt the wolf slide under his skin and he forced it back, clenching his jaw with the effort.

"You know," Jacob said, "You never answered my question yesterday."

"And what question was that?"

"Is she yours?"

Garrett stilled, staring down at the table. Yes!, he thought, just barely managing to hold back a possessive growl. He glanced at Jacob out of the corner of his eye and said, "It's not possible for her to be mine, Jacob."

"Why?"

He laughed. "Why?" he asked, turning to face him. "If you haven't noticed, she's human."

"So?"

"So how exactly am I supposed to claim her as mine?"

Jacob stared at him before shaking his head. "It can be done, Garrett."

"Yeah, if I want to risk the chance of infecting her and I don't. I wouldn't wish this on anyone, accidental or not." He'd spent the night stalking the house with those very thoughts running through his head. He busied himself looking out windows and making sure the doors were all locked. He'd paced the hall, stopped at Rayna's bedroom door and stood there, listening to her breathe. The need to mark her, to make her his, was painful. His teeth ached, his skin tightened and his cock throbbed with the need to do it, especially with so many other wolves near by. If there were a way to stake his claim without infecting her, she'd already be his. But there wasn't.

Checking the table again, Garrett tried to distract his thoughts by making sure everything was there. At the sound of Jacob's laughter, he turned his head. "What?" he snapped.

"Nothing."

"Then why are you laughing?"

Jacob's smile was blinding. "Just never thought I'd see the day when you'd go all moon-eyed over a woman."

"Moon-eyed?" Garrett said, growling at him. "What are you, twelve?"

"Does she know?"

Garrett glanced back down at the table. "No."

"It might be a good time to let her know how you feel about her."

"Why's that?"

"She was all the pack talked about yesterday. They'd been sneaking up to the house all day trying to get a peek at her. If you're too afraid to claim her, I know for a fact there are others who aren't whether she's infected or not."

That piece of information woke his beast. He felt it stir, stretch inside his skin and snap teeth sharp enough to break bones. He turned, crossed the distance separating them in three long strides and stopped in front of him, narrowing his eyes. "Who?"

Jacob leaned back and grinned. "Caleb, for one. He had quite a bit to say about her, actually."

He growled before he could stop himself. Jacob looked over his shoulder then, into the living room, and Garrett did the same. Rayna was walking to the kitchen, a strained smile on her face. Had she heard them? *God, I hope not.*

When she saw them looking at her, she stopped. "What?"

Jacob was the first to speak. "Nothing. Hungry?"

"Famished," she said, crossing to the table and stopping.

"Good. Hope you like omelets."

"I'm so hungry I'd be tempted to eat road kill at the moment."

"Mmmm... sounds tasty," Jacob said, grinning. "You should have told me sooner. I could have whipped that up for you in a flash."

She laughed, her nose crinkling as she did. "I think I'll have the omelet, thank you," she said, taking her seat. "You boys can stick to the raw meat. No offense."

"None taken."

Garrett took the seat across from her and tried not to stare. She seemed happier this morning than she had the night before. Of course, she'd probably been in shock most of the night. She'd nearly passed out when Bryce had shifted, not to mention Malcolm's revelation, her mad dash through the woods to escape the pack and the fright he'd given her when he finally met up with them again. For someone who hadn't known twenty-four hours ago that the world of the supernatural existed, he thought she'd handled it pretty well. Then again, this was Rayna. She was the strongest willed woman he knew. It was part of the reason he'd been drawn to her.

No one spoke as they ate. The clinking of silverware on plates the only sound in the room. When they'd finished and cleaned all the dishes he refilled his coffee cup and leaned back in his chair.

"We need to come up with a plan," Jacob said. "I'm sure Malcolm is forming one of his own as we speak."

The Calling

Garrett glanced up at Rayna, watching her eyes cloud with worry. The scent of her fear filled his mouth a second later and he saw Jacob shift in his seat. "I won't let them hurt you, Rayna. You don't have to be afraid."

"I'm not," she said, pushing her plate away. She looked up and sighed. "Does it show on my face?"

"No. I can smell it," he said.

Her eyes widened a bit. "Smell it? What do you mean?"

"We have a very keen sense of smell," Jacob said.

"Some of us do," Garrett grinned. "Jacob is the exception to the rule."

"Very funny," Jacob said. "I can smell just fine. I know she's scared. She reeks of it."

"Judith mentioned something to me about it," Rayna said. "The smelling fear thing but I didn't really understand what she meant."

Jacob turned to her and leaned his arms on the table. "We can smell fear, just like she said. When your pulse races it causes your scent to thicken in the air and it coats my tongue like thick molasses."

"My scent?"

"Yes. Too bad you smell like Garrett though." He laughed and leaned back in his seat. "I'd much rather taste flowers than him."

Her cheeks reddened and she lifted a hand, pulling the robe she was wearing closed.

"It's the clothes," Garrett said. "My scent is on your skin."

She met his eyes and said, "Oh."

"Not that I'm complaining," he said, grinning. She smiled and ducked her head, lifting her coffee cup and taking a sip. "I'd much rather smell me on you than the pup here."

"Hey," Jacob said. "No name calling before noon. Besides, this *pup* got her to safety while you were busy playing the hero."

"Next time, you can play the hero," Garrett said. "I'd much rather save the girl and hide out for a while. Less painful."

"No thanks," Jacob said. "Unlike you, I'm not crazy enough to go against the entire pack single-handedly. Omega's run when the big boys get all gnarly and besides," he laughed, "I excel at running."

Garrett grinned and looked back at Rayna. She was staring at him and his body tightened at her bold gaze. He inhaled deeply, taking in his scent that lingered on her skin and he wanted nothing more in that moment than to pull her from her chair, sit her on his lap and kiss her until she couldn't breathe. His fantasy was interrupted when Jacob said, "So, what do you think we should do?" He glanced at Jacob and leaned forward, propping his elbows on the table. "Get her out of town. We can't stay here long. The sooner she's gone, the better off we'll be."

"I can't leave without Mitch," Rayna said. "I won't."

He looked up and met her gaze. "Getting you safe is our first priority. We can come back for Mitch."

"Garrett, if they want me bad enough to lure me here what makes you think I'll be safe anywhere I am? Malcolm practically stalked me for six months. They know where I live."

At her words, he saw the torn, ripped body of the young victim lying in the alley in Bluff's Point and knew she was right. He looked up at her and knew his face reflected what he thought.

"What?" she said. He sighed and lowered his head. "Garrett?"

He rubbed a hand over his face and looked up at her. "There isn't a serial killer in Bluff's Point."

"What do you mean? And what does that have to do with this?"

"It has everything to do with this and I know who it is," he said. "Well, not exactly who it is, but I know *what* it is."

"*What* it is," she said, confusion wrinkling her brow. Her eyes widened a moment later. "You mean—"

"A wolf."

"A wolf? As in a werewolf? *That's* what's been killing all those women?" He nodded. "Does the police department know this?"

He snorted a laugh and shook his head. "No. It wasn't exactly something I could tell anyone, now was it?"

She stared at him for long moments before saying, "You know why don't you?" When he didn't answer her, she clenched her jaw and said, "Damn it, Garrett. Now isn't the time for secrets. After last night I wouldn't think you had any more of those. Not any that will shock me more than that one did."

He leaned back and crossed his arms over his chest. "Did you ever follow up on any of the victims?"

"Of course I did," she said. "I always ran an article on the victims."

"Did nothing about those women ever seem familiar to you?"

"Should they have?"

"Think about it, Rayna. Think about each of them and what you learned."

She was quiet, staring at him for over five minutes before her eyes widened. Her face went stark white the next. "He was looking for me, wasn't he?" When he nodded his head at her, she asked, "Why? Why would Malcolm have those women killed if he wanted me to come down here? It makes no sense. Was he trying to turn me into a—"

"I don't think Malcolm is the one who sent the wolf after you."

She shook her head. "I'm confused," she said. "You just said—"

"Someone sent him but it wasn't Malcolm."

"Who then?"

Garrett glanced at Jacob before looking back at her. "Carmen."

Eight

"Carmen?" Rayna said, wide-eyed. "Carmen sent a wolf to kill me? Why?"

He got up from the table, poured his coffee down the sink and walked to the living room.

Rayna stared at him, watching him look out the window. She glanced at Jacob, noticing him look at anything but her before he got up and left the cabin without a word. She stood and crossed the room, stopping just behind Garrett. "Why would Carmen send someone to kill me, Garrett? Yesterday was the first time I've ever met her."

He sighed and leaned against the window. Long minutes passed before he spoke. "I spent five years in Wolf's Creek after I was turned. I was twenty-four, scared out of my fucking head at what I'd become, and these people were all I had in the world. They were like me. Freaks that didn't fit into society. I met Carmen the second day I was here." He turned his head and glanced at her and she knew by the look on his face what he was going to say next. Her stomach cramped at the thought and she hoped she was wrong.

He looked back out the window, fixing his gaze on some distant point and continued. "She was different from anyone I'd ever met. I realize now it was just the wolf in her that made her so..." He shrugged and didn't explain. "But she started to change after a while. Grew more aggressive and talked about overthrowing Malcolm. I didn't think much of it at first. She loved nothing better than a little blood play and I thought she was just being Carmen. When she convinced a few of the other pack members that her plan to overthrow Malcolm was in their best interest, she tried to get me to challenge him. I knew she was serious then."

Rayna ignored the Carmen bit and asked, "What do you mean by challenge him?"

He turned and faced her, leaning his shoulder on the window frame. "Pack hierarchy is based on power. The strongest Alpha in the pack always leads, everyone else follows. It's the way its always been done. In order for someone new to take over, he has to prove to the pack he's strong enough to lead them. Once a challenge is made on the pack leader, they fight until only one remains."

Her eyes widened. "To the death, you mean?"

He nodded. "Most of the time. A pack leader will only relinquish his role by total defeat. He'd be an outcast if he just surrendered and there can only be one leader. Any pack can have any number of Alpha's though. Their strength varies but the strongest always leads."

Rayna shifted on her feet and glanced out the window. "So, Carmen thought you were strong enough to fight Malcolm and win?" she said, looking back up at him.

"I am strong enough to fight Malcolm and win."

She smiled at him and shook her head. "Your arrogance is showing, Garrett. Surely you aren't that confident in your abilities."

"I was stronger than any of them twelve years ago and I've only improved with age." He grinned at her and stood to his full height. "There isn't anyone in Wolf's Creek as strong as me and that isn't arrogance talking, that's fact."

"Okay, so you're the big bad wolf around these parts," she said, rolling her eyes at him. "And Carmen wanted you to prove it. Why? What did she gain by Malcolm being gone?"

"Carmen wanted to lead the pack."

She raised an eyebrow at him and shook her head. "But if you fought Malcolm and won, you'd be pack leader, not her. How would that make her leader?"

"She's Alpha female in Wolf's Creek."

"So?" That look crossed his face again and she knew. "Oh, I see. Whoever fucks the head honcho is at the top of the food chain, right?"

He nodded his head. "The pack leaders mate would also be seen as leader regardless of her rank."

"I see." She stared at him and tried to get the visions of him and Carmen out of her head without much success. She saw her in her mind's eye, saw the smile the woman had given her yesterday and now, the looks she'd caught didn't seem quite so odd. She looked up at Garrett and asked, "Was Carmen trying to get rid of me because of you?"

"I think so," he said.

She laughed and walked closer to him, leaning her shoulder against the wall. "Isn't twelve years quite a long time to hold some torch for a guy who left you?"

"What?" he smiled. "You don't think I'm worth some woman holding a torch for?"

"I haven't seen any proof of it."

"Maybe you haven't been looking in the right places." He glanced down and she followed his gaze, laughing when she realized what he meant.

"All right, enough," she said, waving her hand to dismiss his comment. "We'll debate your *torch* another time, right now, tell me why Carmen waited this long to come after you."

He sobered and shifted his weight, moving closer to her. "I left the pack not long after I realized what Carmen was up to and spent four years roaming the country until I found Bluff's Point. Eight years later, she finally tracked me down. When she tried to get me to come back and fight Malcolm, I refused. Carmen likes to have her way so she paid me a visit to try and lure me back the only way she knows how."

"What? She was going to fuck you into submission?"

"Something like that."

She stared at him, visions of him and Carmen once again filling her head. She didn't like the visual or the fact that the woman had gone so far just to try and seduce him. *Is that all she did, though? Try?* "Carmen was in Bluff's Point?"

"Yes."

Rayna crossed her arms under her breasts and leaned her head to one side. "Before or after there was an us?"

He paused and then said, "During."

Her pulse leaped and a lump formed in her throat. Why did he pause like that? "Did you sleep with her when she was there?"

"No," he said, his voice strong and sure. "I haven't been with anyone else since the day I met you."

"Are you lying?"

His eyes widened and his face turned red. "What reason do I have to lie to you?"

"To save your ass?" she said, jealousy making her words clipped. "Getting caught with your dick in some ho would make even a saint lie."

"I haven't touched her since the day I left this place, Rayna. Believe me or not."

She wanted to believe him but she'd seen Carmen. The woman was exotic looking and had a body even she would kill to have. She could see her seducing anyone she wanted to and she probably did.

"Rayna."

She focused her gaze on him and sighed, waving her hand to dismiss the whole issue. "It doesn't matter now anyway," she said, not happy about it but what could she do? Nothing. "So, when Carmen found out you weren't interested, as you say, what?"

"I wasn't interested," he said, giving her a pointed look. "And she found out why when she saw me with you."

"I see. So, what, in a jealous rage she sent some crazed werewolf to get rid of me?"

"No, she threatened to kill you herself." Chills raced down her spine at that. She'd been in the same room with a woman who wanted her dead? "Luckily for you she was more afraid of me than she was of risking her own neck. She left saying I'd come crawling to her before it was all said and done. The threat was there, as flimsy as it was, but it was enough. I broke it off with you and tried to keep you far enough away no one would link me to you."

"And then the first body turned up."

He nodded. "I didn't put the pieces together until the third one. When I looked at all three victims and realized they were all brunettes and twenty-nine, I immediately thought of you. When I saw they graduated from Hamilton, I knew whoever was killing those women wasn't your average serial killer. The method of death was too brutal for a human so I started looking harder. That's when I smelled the wolf on the victims and knew whoever it was, was looking for you."

"So you tore my heart out and stomped on it every chance you got so Carmen's pet werewolf wouldn't find me?" He didn't answer but she saw the truth of her words on his face. He left her, and treated her like shit, to protect her. She didn't know whether she should kiss him or kick his ass.

"What are you thinking?" he asked.

"You don't want to know."

"That bad?"

She smiled and looked away, leaning back against the wall. "I don't know what to think."

"Do you want to know what I think?" He reached out and hooked a finger under her chin, turning her head toward him. "I think, now that everything is out in the open, I don't have a reason to push you away anymore."

She stared up at him and narrowed her eyes. "Oh, so now that I know your secret, one you didn't trust me enough to tell me to begin with, everything is fine? That I should just forget what an asshole you've been to me for the last six months? Is that what you think?"

He smiled. "Yeah, that's what I think."

Why was he smiling? Did he honestly think she was just going to forgive him just like that? Of course he did. She laughed and shook her head, dislodging his hand from her face. "You are the biggest horses' ass I've ever known, Garrett Kincaid! All those poor, innocent rabbits you slaughter while all furry have rotted your brain."

"Maybe, but you still want me."

She snorted. "In your dreams."

His arm shot out, lightening quick, and wrapped around her waist, jerking her to him. He raised his other hand, cupping her cheek before working his fingers into her hair. "Always," he said, leaning down to kiss her. He licked her bottom lip, forcing his tongue inside her mouth and she went limp in his arms. Just like the night before when he'd kissed her, she lost all reason to think. The only thing that registered was the incredible heat from his body, his scent and the feel of his mouth on hers. Tingles raced laps up and down her spine as she reached up, wrapping her arms around his neck while her stomach clenched in anticipation. Asshole he may be but her body hummed with the knowledge of the things he could do, the things he could make her feel and she cursed herself for a fool as she moaned into his mouth and pushed her hips against him, trying to get closer.

He broke the kiss and looked down at her. "Your fear isn't the only thing I can smell, Rayna." He smiled and inhaled deeply, his eyes closing briefly. "I can smell how much you want me."

"Smell…" Her eyes widened when she realized what he meant. There was no denying how her body reacted to him. "Oh," she said. "And eww. Don't be smelling me like that."

He laughed, kissed her lightly on the lips and brushed his own across her cheek. "There's nothing 'eww' about it," he said, kissing her jaw before working his way down the side of her neck. "Being able to tell from across the room how much you want me does more than just stroke my ego. It makes me want to throw you to the nearest hard surface I can find and fuck you until you're screaming my name. Do you have any idea what the scent of you does to the wolf?"

"No," she whispered, tilting her head to one side, her eyes closing as he peppered kisses along her skin.

"He wants you as much as I do. Wants to claim you. Make you his and his alone."

Rayna opened her eyes and turned her head to look at him. "Claim me? What do you mean?"

The door opened and Jacob, breathless, rushed inside the cabin. "We have company."

Garrett let go of her as if he'd been burned and turned to the window. "How many?"

"More than you can take on by yourself."

Garrett turned and looked at her, their intimate moment forgotten. "Go put your clothes on. Be ready to run in less than five."

She nodded her head and ran, darting into the laundry room and snatching her clothes out of the dryer. She stripped, not caring if anyone saw her, and jerked her clothes on before running back to the living room and grabbing her sneakers. Her hands were shaking and she tried to calm down, looking up when she'd slid her feet into her shoes and stood. "What are we going to do?"

The Calling

Garrett turned to look at her. "You, are going to go out the back with Jacob," he said. Turning to look at Jacob, he said, "Get her to my truck and get as far away from here as you can."

"And what about you?" she said.

"Don't worry about me." He turned from the window and walked across the room, grabbing his own shoes. "If you can't outrun them, Jacob, then don't do anything stupid. They want her alive but you, I don't think they'll care too much about."

"Gee, thanks," Jacob said, but smiled as he did. "I can lose them. I know these woods like the back of my hand."

Garrett nodded and stood, walking back across the room. He reached the door before Rayna yelled, "Wait!" She crossed the room to him, grabbing his arm and said, "What are you going to do?"

He turned and looked at her, giving her a faint smile. "What I do best," he said. "Now go with Jacob. I'll come for you as soon as I get rid of the welcoming party." He kissed her, hard and fast, and turned back to the door.

"Garrett?"

He turned his head and smiled. "It'll be fine, Rayna."

"How? How can it be fine? You don't even know how many are out there."

"They'll not attack unless they have to and as long as you're gone it won't make much difference if they do."

So he was just going to offer himself up as bait? I don't think so! She clenched her teeth and gave him a look she hoped let him know she was serious. "You walk out that door, Garrett Kincaid, and I swear I'll be one step behind you."

He let go of the doorknob and gave her a look that chilled her to the bone. "No, you won't."

Rayna lifted her chin, ignoring his heated glare. "And how are you going to stop me?"

She actually heard his teeth grind as he clenched his jaw and stared at her. It took seconds for him to go from pissed off to furious. When he advanced on her, she held her ground, but just barely. "You *will* go with Jacob. You will get into my truck and head away from Wolf's Creek and if I find out you've done anything other than that, you *will* need to run. From me."

"I'm not scared of you," she said, hoping he didn't hear her voice tremble. "And I'm not leaving this house without you."

His expression turned to stone and his warm, honey brown eyes bled to wolf amber. She could hear a soft rumbling come from his chest. Not exactly a growl but... something. He didn't say anything but continued to stare at her until she wanted to slink away unseen. She swallowed the lump forming in her throat and tried to sound braver than she felt. "You wouldn't let them do anything to hurt me and I'm not going to allow them to hurt you because of me. Either you come with us or I stay. Your choice."

"I'm not running from them, Rayna."

"Then run *with* me," she said. "If your pride is all that's keeping you from tucking tail, then *you* get me out of here. Don't leave my safety in Jacob's hands."

The Calling

He glanced at Jacob for brief seconds before looking back down at her. "Why are you so fucking stubborn?"

"The same reason your so fucking cocky. We were born that way."

His mouth twitched in one corner and if she hadn't been staring at him, she would have never seen it. He blew out a breath before looking over her head to Jacob. "Go see if it's all clear out back."

When Jacob left the room, Garrett grabbed her, pulling her flush up against him. "Don't think you can bully me into doing everything you want, Rayna."

She smiled and leaned up on her toes, kissing him soundly on the mouth. "Then don't think you can bully me into doing everything you want. Just because you can go all furry doesn't make you boss. Even old dogs can be taught new tricks." He did growl then and she kissed him again for good measure before pulling herself from his arms and grabbed his hand, turning and starting toward the back of the house.

Jacob was staring out the window when they stopped behind him and he eased the door open. "It's clear," he said. "No movement and I don't smell anyone."

Garrett put his hand on her shoulder and eased her toward the door. "What's the shortest path to the creek?"

"The shortest isn't the best," he said. "If we head toward the upper ridge first, we can lose them in the brush. Remember how it smells up there?"

Garrett nodded and his nose crinkled. "Which way?"

"Run straight for the woodshed," Jacob said. "There's a path just behind it. When it veers to the left, turn right, through the brush. There's no path but keep a straight line and we'll be fine."

Rayna nodded and peeked out the door. The shed was on the left side of the house, half hidden by a dense growth of trees. Her heart was in her throat and she swallowed to get the lump forming to clear. Garrett gave her one last look before placing his hand on her back and nodding to Jacob, who slung the door open.

Her feet hit the planks on the porch hard and she jumped the step to the ground, running hell bent for the woodshed. When she was behind it, she turned her head to see if Garrett was indeed following her and froze. She had a perfect view of the front of the cabin and what she saw nearly stopped her heart. Dozens of people were lined along the trees and the number of wolves was too numerous to count. Seeing them the night before had scared her, seeing them in the light of day terrified the hell out of her. They ranged in colors from black to red, gold and brown. They were all huge; those on four legs were crouched low to the ground and the ones standing erect towered to dizzying heights.

Jacob finally ran behind the shed, Garrett right behind him. She turned, running for the trail and hoped like hell Garrett was still with her. She'd kick his ass if he ditched her now. Jacob took the lead and she could hear the heavy footfalls of Garrett behind her. She ran until her lungs ached from the effort and her muscles burned from exertion trying to keep up with Jacob with not much luck. He darted through the vegetation like a spry rabbit, dodging trees and logs, jumping them with an ease born of a creature used to the forest. A fallen tree limb buried in the underbrush caught her foot, tripping her, and she tried not to scream as she fell. Garrett caught her before she hit the ground.

"Are you all right?" he asked.

She panted for breath and nodded her head at him. He wasn't even winded, she noticed. He smiled and said, "Do you trust me?" She wanted to say, "Of course," but couldn't get enough air into her lungs to do so.

He winked at her and she managed a small squeak when he grabbed her and lifted her off the ground. She barely got her arms around his neck before he was running again.

Rayna held on, burying her face in his neck as the trees sped by in a blur. Her stomach felt queasy as she watched them and eventually closed her eyes as he raced through the forest.

The faint sound of running water reached her long minutes later and Garrett slowed before coming to a complete stop. Rayna lifted her head, looking behind them and saw nothing but forest. Looking at Jacob she saw him turning in a circle with an odd look on his face. When he turned toward them, she knew something was wrong. "What is it?"

"Shh," Garrett said, his hold on her tightening. He turned his head, scanning the forest and her heart raced when he eased her to the ground. "Go to Jacob," he said, quietly.

She didn't argue. Jacob grabbed her arm the moment she reached him and pulled her close to his body. Like Garrett, he was barely winded but he held himself as stiff as Garrett was. They sensed something she couldn't.

Looking up at him confirmed it. His gaze was fixed over the rise, and she turned her head to look. Movement in the trees, brief flashes of shapes darted amongst the brush and when she saw the first wolf jump toward them, she screamed.

Jacob grabbed her with both hands, one over her mouth, before he turned, looking behind him and started pulling her away. She screamed into his hand, her heels scoring the ground as the area filled with wolves. When the first howl echoed through the trees, she looked toward Garrett, her eyes widening as she encountered a sight she never wanted to see.

He was changing. Shifting into the wolf.

Tears burnt her eyes as she watched his bones shift under his skin, lengthening and reshaping, his flesh convulsing as the clear liquid she'd seen on Bryce dripped and slid off his body. Thick hair grew in wild patches, racing down his limbs, his clothes ripping as he grew larger. His face contorted, his mouth elongating as teeth sharp enough to break bones sprang forth. He lifted his head and howled, the sound causing every hair on her body to stand on end. She was crying in earnest by the time Jacob picked her up and darted through the trees, away from Garrett and the dozens of wolves he faced alone.

Nine

Rayna sat huddled under a thick clump of brush. She barely smelled the pungent odor it gave off. Her head was too stopped up from crying for her to smell much of anything. Her eyes still burned and itched and the tremble in her limbs hadn't stopped. She couldn't get the sight of Garrett shifting out of her head no matter how hard she tried. Knowing what he was and seeing him like that was one thing. Watching as his body transformed right in front of her was another. It had scared the hell out of her when Bryce had done it in Malcolm's little demonstration.

Watching Garrett do it terrified her beyond reason.

She glanced toward Jacob. He was sitting close to her, his eyes scanning the area. He looked ready to jump out of his skin. She swallowed and sniffed, wishing she had a tissue before wiping her face dry. "Do you think he's all right?" she whispered.

"Yes," he said, without looking at her. "Don't worry about him so much. You'll bruise his ego if he finds out." He turned his head and smiled at her and she knew he was trying to make light of the situation. She wanted to thank him for it but it didn't erase the fear. "What are we going to do?"

He shook his head. "That's a very good question," he said. He turned to face her, sitting down and wrapping his arms around his knees. "I can't take them on myself," he said. "I can, but it won't do either of us any good, especially me." He grinned at her and hugged his legs tighter. "They'd wipe the floor with my ass. I'm what they refer to as an Omega. I'm the lowest member of the pack, the weakest, if you will. The majority of the others are Beta's. They're stronger than me but nothing compared to the Alpha's. So, I can try to fight our way out if we're found but the only thing it's going to do is prove to you how utterly unsafe you are in my care."

"So you're saying we just hide then?"

"Unless you have a better idea," he said. "They won't be able to find us here, though. The odor these plants give off will mask our scent. As long as we stay still, they'd have to trip over us to find us."

"Will they be able to hear us?"

"If they're close enough," he said. "The rushing water from the creek will tune us out a bit."

Rayna fell silent, her mind going in so many directions she didn't know which path to take. Fear was still eating at her nerves and she sighed before wrapping her arms around her legs and laying her head on her knees. She stared at Jacob, taking in his youthful appearance. She couldn't imagine him a wolf. He was tall and gangly and imagining him as one of those massive creatures was mind-boggling.

She closed her eyes, again seeing Garrett in her mind's eye. Her pulse leaped as she recalled seeing him change and she wasn't sure she'd ever get that image out of her head. When Bryce had shifted, his screams had nearly done her in. It was a slow and agonizing process to watch. When Garrett had shifted, it looked like the most natural thing in the world. He hadn't screamed at all and the change took him so quickly she would have missed it had she turned her head. But seeing him shift had cemented the fact of what he was into her head. There was no way for her to deny it no matter how much she wanted to. Garrett was a werewolf. A big, mean, scary looking son of a bitch. She shuddered and hugged her knees tighter as his wolf image filled her head.

"The chances of them finding us here are slim."

"I wasn't thinking about the others," she said.

"Well, you certainly don't have a reason to be afraid of Garrett."

She opened her eyes and looked up when Jacob's softly spoken words reached her. "I'm not," she lied.

He smiled and shifted on the ground. "He wouldn't hurt you. Ever."

"I know that," she said.

"You know *Garrett* wouldn't hurt you but you don't know his wolf. That, you're afraid of."

"Let me guess," she said. "The smelling thing again?" He grinned. "That's really creepy, you know."

He shrugged a shoulder. "If you say so."

The images were still there and she couldn't shake them. She stared at Jacob, trying to imagine what he looked like as a wolf and decided to ask. "What kind are you?"

"What do you mean?"

"Well, I saw other wolves like Garrett," she said. "He was on two legs but there's others, they resembled real wolves, only bigger. Which are you?"

"Oh. I'm a four-legger," he grinned. "I'm not strong enough to do a fancy half-shift."

"That's what it is?"

"Yes. The strong ones, the Alpha's, can control how much they actually shift. It's why they stay erect and can still talk. The weaker ones have no control so we end up on all fours."

"So Garrett can actually shift and end up on four legs like the others?"

"Yes. He just chooses not to. Most of the Alpha's don't. It makes it easier to fight when you have use of your arms."

"Does it hurt?"

"Does what hurt?"

"When you change?"

He nodded. "Yeah. Hurts like a bitch. All those howls you hear when we shift aren't for show. It's a necessity. Enough pain will make even the strongest man scream."

"Garrett didn't."

Jacob laughed. "That's because he's an arrogant bastard who wouldn't show anyone his pain if they cut both his damn legs off."

Rayna smiled at that. It sounded just like Garrett. Always the bad ass no matter what the circumstances. Still, watching him change, bravely or not, would haunt her for months. "You said shift. Is that the correct term for it?"

"Yes. A change is just going from one thing to another," he said, "What we do is shift our physical shape. It's where the term shape-shifter came from."

The Calling

She shook her head. "Do you have any idea how hard all this is to take in?"

"About as hard as it is to accept when you wake up one day and you're no longer what you used to be."

She made a non-committal noise in the back of her throat and looked out through the bushes. The sun was setting and a glance at her watch told her they'd been hiding for close to an hour. "Where do you think he is?" He didn't answer. "Do you think he's all right?"

"Yes, for the second time. I'm sure he's fine." He chuckled and shook his head. "You know, for someone who looked ready to pee her pants the first time you saw him you act awfully concerned."

"Well, he's still Garrett under all that hair."

"Remember that the next time he's right in front of you," he said. "The wolf wants you. If you get skittish around him, it'll just make Garrett feel like shit. He might look different but Garrett is still in there. He sees everything. He hears what you say and he can smell your fear. Fear of him."

She looked away and thought about what he said, trying to ignore the part where her fear might actually hurt Garrett. As much as he'd hurt her in the past, she didn't want to do the same to him. She sighed and looked up, tilting her head. "Garrett told me the wolf wanted me, too," she said, trying to shift her thoughts. "What did he mean by that exactly?"

Jacob's cheeks reddened before he cleared his throat. "Well, just like every other creature on the planet, the wolf will search out a mate, just like humans do."

"A mate? You mean a girlfriend?" She laughed and shook her head. "Why would his wolf want me for a girlfriend?"

"Why wouldn't he?"

"I'm not a werewolf."

"So. The wolf finding a mate isn't just about the sex."

The visual she got then made her own cheeks redden. Her face flamed before she looked away. She heard Jacob chuckle before he said, "What you do with the wolf is entirely up to you and before you ask, yes, I do know of wolves who engage in sex acts with humans. It's not for everyone but to each his own."

She gaped at him. "Humans and wolves having sex?"

He grinned and shrugged his shoulders. "Our parts still work after the shift and a woman is a woman, no matter what she looks like."

She didn't even want to go there. Accepting the fact Garrett was a wolf was hard enough. Thinking about… that, was a stretch even she couldn't make and never would. "Okay, so if I'm not willing to have sex with Garrett's wolf, then why would it want me?"

"I told you," he said. "It's not about the sex. It's no different than why you hooked up with Garrett to begin with. It's about attraction and desire. The wolf wants you for his own. Plain and simple."

"But if Garrett has me then doesn't the wolf?"

"No," he said. "Not really. It's an entirely different thing for a man to have you than for a wolf to. Humans, when they decide to make it permanent, get married. Wolves, claim a mate. Mark them so others can see."

The Calling

"Mark them? Like a dog marking his territory?" She laughed and pushed her hair out of her face. "This is unreal."

Jacob laughed. "It's no where near the same thing," he said. "A claim is a very powerful thing. It isn't just about saying you belong to him and him alone. It's about protection and the desire to see to a mates needs above his own. Another wolf wouldn't even attempt to harm another wolf's mate unless he knew without a doubt he could fight him and win, cause anyone crazy enough to fuck with a wolf's mate will basically sign his death warrant. If Garrett's wolf had claimed you already, we wouldn't be sitting under this foul smelling ragweed. No one would be crazy enough to come after you knowing Garrett's wolf would rip their throat out for even looking at you funny."

"Well if it's that damn simple, why hasn't he done it yet? Malcolm will back off, right?"

"But it's not simple," he said. "The claim isn't. He has to mark you and that means a physical mark. Bites most of the time. It's easy for one wolf to claim another, not so much when it's a wolf and a human, not to mention that once a claim is made, it can't be broken. It isn't like you can divorce a wolf once the claim is made. Wolves mate for life and there's no going back. Even if you decide later on you don't want Garrett, the wolf won't just back away. He may let you go but you can damn sure bet he won't go far. He'll follow you to the day you die."

She let his words run through her head. Lifelong mates and bites the most prevailing thought. Looking back up at him she said, "If a human is bit by a werewolf, they can be turned, right?"

He nodded his head.

"So Garrett can infect me if the wolf bites me during the claiming?"

"Infection isn't always the case, but it's a big enough risk that Garrett isn't willing to take it no matter how much he wants to, and believe me, he wants to." He turned, peeking out through the brush before looking up at the sky. He stared at the surrounding forest for long minutes before turning back to face her. "I haven't heard anything since we jumped in here. Ready to make another run for it?"

"Yes," she said, unfolding her arms from around her legs. "My ass has gone numb from sitting so long."

"All right," he said. "Just stick close to me. We don't have much further to go to reach Garrett's truck."

They climbed out and took a moment to stretch, Jacob scanning the forest again. When he was happy no one was around he grabbed her hand and once again, they were running.

Malcolm knew by the look on Caleb's face things hadn't gone as planned. That and the fact he didn't have Rayna with him. He scowled and leaned back in his chair. "What happened?"

Caleb growled and kicked a chair out from under the table and sat down. "Those pathetic dogs you sent with me all ran with their tails between their legs two minutes after Garrett shifted and took the first swing at one of them. Apparently knowing he killed two of us already and injured a dozen more was enough for them to piss themselves at the sight of him."

"Well I'm going to assume you didn't run."

"Of course I didn't," he said.

"And?" Malcolm said.

"And nothing. We both live to fight another day."

"And the girl?"

"She took off with Jacob. I sent a group after them and either they didn't find them or they used it as an excuse to run like the others did."

Malcolm stared at Caleb and wondered what to do now. Caleb was the best fighter he had next to himself. If he couldn't subdue Garrett alone and no one was willing to stand with him, they didn't have much chance in getting Rayna away from him. He needed another plan and fast. "I'll think of something," he said. "In the meantime, I'd like for you to speak to Carmen."

Caleb raised an eyebrow at him. "About what?"

"I think she's the reason Garrett is here."

"She's not still pining over him, if that's what you think. That's ancient history."

"Then how did Garrett know Rayna was here?"

Caleb shrugged his shoulder. "He was fucking her for months. Maybe he still is."

"And maybe Carmen is scheming behind my back," he said, anger lacing his words. "This plan was her idea. She said Ms. Ford was the best choice for being our spokesperson but I'm beginning to think she has ulterior motives. As my second in command, I want you to find out. If she lured Garrett down here for her own selfish reasons and ruins our chance at this, I'll rip her heart out and feed it to the crows. Now go and see what you can find out."

Caleb stood and walked out of the room, climbing the steps to the second story. He could smell Carmen's perfume from the top of the stairs and knew without being told she was entertaining the newest member of the pack. When he opened the bedroom door and saw her, naked and stretched out on top of Mitch, he laughed. "Couldn't wait, could you?"

"He's tasty," Carmen said, leaning down and licking the side of the man's neck. "And his cock is fat, just the way I like them."

The look on Mitch's face was comical at best. Fear was shining in his eyes but the lust he couldn't deny rode him hard. His dick was at attention and Caleb knew no matter what Carmen did to the man, he'd stay that way. She had certain talents no man could resist.

"Did you come to watch or join us," she said, rising to her knees and straddling Mitch's chest.

"Neither. Malcolm sent me up here."

She looked at him and smiled. "Does he know I'm up here?"

"No and I don't really think he'd care one way or the other if he did."

Carmen scowled. "You'd think after making the old goat come as hard as I do he'd be at least a little jealous."

"If he cared about you in the least, he might."

She growled and Caleb saw Mitch tense under her, pulling on his restraints. "He thinks you called Garrett and told him of the plan."

The Calling

"Does he now," she said, smiling. "Did he tell you that?"

"Yes. He also told me to find out if it's true."

"Then tell him it isn't."

Caleb grinned at her and walked to the bed. "And what do I get for saving your ass again?"

"What would you like, lover?"

He looked down at Mitch and grinned. "A game," he said.

"Are you going to join us?"

He nodded his head and pulled his shirt up over his head and tossed it to the floor before unfastening his pants. "Always," he said. "But first, I want you to shift and ride him. I want to hear him scream."

Ten

Rayna jumped when Jacob kicked the side of Garrett's truck, his foot denting the door. Not that it mattered with the way the truck looked now. All four tires were shredded, every window was busted out and it looked as if someone took a can opener and peeled back the metal on both sides. She didn't have to be told that the wolves who'd been hunting them destroyed their only means of escape. "What now," she asked.

Jacob laughed but she could tell it was out of desperation, not humor. "I have no fucking clue," he said. "I just hope Garrett finds us before the others do."

She glanced around, a chill running up her spine as she stared into the forest. "You don't think they're still here, do you?"

"No. If they were they would have made themselves known by now."

She watched him stalk to the creek bank and bend down, scooping a handful of water into his hands and splashing it onto his face and neck. He sat there for long minutes staring at the water before standing and walking back to the truck. He opened the doors, rummaging around inside before saying, "Ah, Garrett, you clever bastard." He turned and handed her a blanket before continuing his search. "There's camping gear in here. Luckily for us, Garrett still knows how to live prepared for anything," he said. "Too bad he didn't stash any food, though. I'm half starved." He straightened, another blanket in his arms.

Rayna hugged the blanket he'd handed her to her chest and glanced around the clearing. "I take it we're camping then?"

"Unless you want to hike back to the cabin?"

The thought of that caused her to shudder. "No. I don't want to chance running into one of those wolves out there in the dark."

The area they were in was pretty open. She could see a faint trail that could have been a road but the grass camouflaged it enough to make it appear as nothing but a beaten path. Why Garrett even parked here was a mystery. It was nowhere near the cabin.

Walking around the truck, she spotted a large oak near the tree line with a bed of grass just under its branches. It looked as good a spot as any and she crossed to it before spreading the blanket out and sitting down, using the tree as a backrest. She'd just got settled when she heard a rustling behind her. When she saw Jacob turn and start toward her, she jumped to her feet and ran to him, hiding like a scared cat behind his back. She peeked over his shoulder and stared into the forest.

Her pulse leaped and her heart slammed against her ribcage when she saw the wolf standing behind the tree she'd been leaning against. Her knees went weak. She'd been that close to the thing and hadn't even known it?

She watched it and poked Jacob in the back when he did nothing but stand there staring. When the wolf stepped out from behind the tree and Jacob's body relaxed, she realized it must be Garrett.

Jacob turned and said, "It's Garrett," and walked away without another word.

The sun hadn't set completely and unlike the night before in the darkened, derelict cabin, Rayna could see Garrett clearly now. The hair covering his body was jet black and shined in the light making it appear almost blue in places. It looked soft and thick and those amber eyes glowed eerily out of the wolf's darkened face. He walked closer and her gaze covered every inch of him. He was impossibly tall, his legs bent at the knees as if he were stooping but she could tell he wasn't. His arms were long and his hands still looked somewhat human. Well, aside from all the hair and the very sharp looking claws. The face, however, didn't look human. It resembled more of a wolf's. His mouth was elongated with a maw she was sure held razor sharp teeth. His ears were long and laid slightly back, relaxed, on his head. He was watching her and still as death. Nothing on him moved and she found it more terrifying than if he'd been moving. Anything that could remain that still wasn't natural.

Well, hello. Werewolf. Not exactly natural, now is it?

"I'm not going to hurt you."

She jumped, startled, when he spoke and her heart resumed racing. His words were somewhat garbled but she still understood him. The fact he was talking to her at all while looking like that was mind numbing. She smiled at him to try and cover her fear and moved back, away from the truck and toward the creek when he took a step toward her. When she was as far as she could get

The Calling

without crossing the creek, he walked completely into the clearing.

The need to cry was overwhelming as she stared at him. Her heart felt like it was breaking. This terrifyingly scary creature was Garrett. Her Garrett. A man she'd been falling in love with before he decided he could no longer have her. A man who left her because of what he was. What he still is. A werewolf. It was too unbelievable for words. She prayed she was going to wake up any moment and be back in Bluff's Point, standing behind a police line watching him work and trying to get his attention while he ignored her.

He turned his head away from her and walked to the truck. She could tell he was pissed by the time he reached it. His ears were standing erect; his back was slightly arched with fur bristled. A snarl eased past a curled lip and she saw the sharp point of his teeth.

Jacob rounded the truck and stopped beside him, laying his hands on the bent metal. "Do you want to hike out of here tonight or wait until sunrise?"

Garrett looked up, staring into the darkening sky before turning to look at her. She was still cowering near the creek bank and when his gaze fell upon her it took everything in her not to take another step backwards. "We'll leave at first light," he said.

Jacob nodded. "I found the blankets and other gear in your truck but not any food. Feel like going on a little hunt for us? None of us have eaten since breakfast."

A nod was all she saw before Garrett turned and ran back into the forest. When he was out of sight, she released the breath she'd been holding. When Jacob turned to look at her, she knew what he was going to say before he even opened his mouth. "It's still Garrett."

"I know," she said, weakly.

"Then stop being so damn scared of him. You're stinking the whole clearing up and I for one don't have Garrett's control. That fear of yours smells like food to me." He turned and left her standing there feeling properly chastised. If Jacob smelled her fear, no doubt Garrett did. She sighed and walked back to her tree, waiting for Garrett to come back. Like it or not, she was going to have to overcome her fear of him. She couldn't have the man without the beast and she wasn't ready to give him up when it looked as if he was willing to give them a second chance. Scared shitless or not, she would make herself accept the furry side of him.

When Garrett returned, he threw several fat rabbits at Jacob's feet and turned, running back into the forest. He didn't even glance in her direction. That was over two hours ago. They'd cleaned the rabbits, cooked them over a fire and as much as she loathed the thought of eating them, she was too hungry to refuse. The meat was dry and rather bland but her stomach had stopped growling. True dark had fallen over the clearing and the stars twinkling overhead were bright. The moon, one day past full, lit the entire area. Jacob was sitting by the fire, feeding twigs into it. He hadn't said anything to her since he'd put her in her place and for some reason, knowing

The Calling

Garrett was avoiding her and now Jacob was refusing to speak, she felt like she was completely alone.

Grabbing the ends of the blanket she was sitting on, she pulled it up, wrapping it around her shoulders. The air had cooled, just as Jacob had said it would, and no matter how tired she was, closing her eyes was impossible. The slightest noise and she was searching the dark for the source of it.

A splash from the creek caused her to turn her head and she searched the creek bed. She saw nothing and leaned back, glancing in one direction to the other. When she looked back to her right, she saw him. Garrett was sitting near the stream further up the creek.

He was staring at her. Those amber wolf eyes glowing in the darkness.

She watched him for long moments, her pulse leaping to rapid life. How long had he been there? Hiding in the dark. Hiding from her. Her chest ached at the thought. As much as she feared him, she didn't want to alienate him and make him feel unwanted. She wanted him near her no matter what he looked like.

It's now or never, she thought, standing and wrapping the blanket around her shoulders. She started toward him, her breaths coming more rapid as she drew closer. When she was close enough to see his face clearly, he stood up.

She froze.

"I won't hurt you, Rayna."

The sound of her name in that deep, garbled baritone sent a chill up her spine. "I know you won't."

"Then come here."

Her hands started shaking at his request. She took two small steps, pausing briefly before taking a few more. Her knees were weak and barely holding her up by the time she reached him. When she stopped in front of him she looked up… and up. He was enormous.

He squatted, bringing him closer to eye level with her, but she still had to lift her head to see his face. He didn't make any other moves and she was shaking so badly she knew he could hear her bones rattling.

"Come here," he said, holding out his hand to her. She stared at it, noticing again how long and sharp the claws were and willed the fear choking her away. She closed the remaining distance between them, stopping directly in front of him. He never moved, didn't make any attempt to touch her, and after long minutes of staring at his outstretched hand, Rayna reached out and touched him.

A quick glance at his face and she knew he wasn't going to do anything but sit there. He was still again, like he had been earlier, and with another bravely fought step toward him, she laid her hand flat in his palm.

Rayna took a shaky breath and stared down at their hands. Hers looked tiny compared to his and she was sure if he closed his fist, he could break her bones without any effort. She moved her hand, sliding it across his palm before tracing the long line of his fingers to the claws at the end. She reached out with her other hand, glancing up at him before turning his hand over. The hair wasn't soft as she imagined. It felt wiry but was thick, even on his hand. Another step forward, her hands tracing the line of his arm, her fingers climbing into the thick nap of hair. She looked up then and noticed how close she was. Another step and she would be able to lean against his chest. He was staring down at her, again still as death, and she wondered what he was thinking. "I'm sorry I'm so scared," she whispered. "I don't mean to be."

"It's fine."

"No, it's not," she said. "I shouldn't be. I know its you in there but…" She raised her hand, touching the side of his face. His eyes closed, his breath leaving in a rush and she felt it hot and moist against her face. She raised both arms, the blanket falling from her shoulders as she explored him, her hands traveling over his wolf form and with every passing second, the fear lessoned.

Her gaze ran over him as her hands stroked him, a small rumbling in his chest telling her more than words how pleased he was. She glanced down the line of his body and blushed. His genitals were very much human-like in appearance and even though she was barely touching him, he looked happy for her to be doing so. She looked back at his face. His eyes were still closed and she leaned toward him, letting her body touch his. "Garrett."

His eyes opened when she said his name and even though no discernable expression could be seen on his face, she could tell her being so close was a relief to him. He stared at her before lifting his arm, the back of one clawed finger running over her hair. She continued to stroke him, to feel his wiry hair between her fingers and the small touches slowly eased the last of her fear.

Closing the remaining distance between them, she leaned against him and turned her head, laying her cheek to his shoulder. She let out the breath she'd been holding when his arms wound around her. As odd as it was to be in the embrace of a creature who could snap her in two, in her mind's eye she saw Garrett, the man, not the impossibly scary wolf he appeared to be.

"The fear is gone," he said.

She smiled. "Let me guess," she said, her eyes still closed. "You don't smell it?"

Another rumble from his massive chest vibrated through her body. "No. I don't smell it. I only smell you." She felt her hair move before feeling the weight of his head against her own, his breath hot against the back of her neck. She was completely surrounded by him, trapped within his arms and she nuzzled her face against him. As scary as the wolf was, she felt safe in his arms. Protected.

"I'm going to assume you won the fight with Caleb and the others?" He made a sound that strongly resembled a laugh. She looked up at him and smiled. "I take that as a yes?"

"They ran."

"They ran?" she said, before laughing. "All that growling and posturing and they ran?"

"All but Caleb. He would never run from a fight."

"And what happened?"

"Nothing. He talked more than anything."

"Brave enough to stay but too scared to fight?" His lip curled up and she knew he was smiling. Still arrogant as ever. "How long do you stay like this?" she asked, running her hands down his arms.

"For as long as I want."

"You can change back anytime you want to?"

"Yes."

"Then why are you still like this?"

"In case they come back," he said. "Once I change, I won't be able to shift back into the wolf for a while. I'll be too weak to even try."

"Do you think they'll come back tonight?"

He looked up and scanned the clearing. "I'm not going to take any chances that they will."

"Do you think they'll come back tonight?" she asked again.

"No."

"They why stay like this?"

"Why not?"

She raised her arm and laid her hand to the side of his face. "Because I want you back."

He stared down at her for long moments before dropping his arms. "If they come back and take you while I can do nothing but watch, I'll let them eat you."

She grinned. "I'd much rather have you eat me... but if that's your choice."

The rumbling in his chest turned to a growl and his lips curled back, revealing those teeth she'd been curious about. "Don't tease a wolf, Rayna, especially a jealous one." Laughing, she stepped back, picking up the blanket. He stood to his full height and backed up several steps. "I'll go to the trees. It'll take a while before I can come back."

"You don't have to leave."

"Are you okay to watch?"

"Not really but I'd rather see it than wonder about it."

He nodded his head and stepped back several more steps. When he'd put enough distance between them, she saw him take several deep breaths before closing his eyes.

The first flicker of movement she saw was the small wave the hair on his body made. It moved and shimmered before slowly receding. The sound of his pained moans was heard, then the audible crack of shifting bones. She saw them then, sliding under his flesh and in a complete reversal of the process she'd watched earlier, the beast slowly slid away and the man came screaming back into focus.

Garrett fell to his hands and knees, his naked body glistening in the moonlight. She ran to him, dropping to her knees in front of him and it wasn't until he lifted his head and looked up at her that she realized she was crying. "Are you all right?"

He nodded and lowered his head again, taking several deep breaths before sitting up on his knees and bracing his hands on his naked thighs. His eyes were still closed and a pained expression covered his face. She looked him over, lifting her hand to rub the side of his face. "Ugh, your skin is slimy."

He smiled with his eyes closed. "A shower usually gets rid of it."

She snarled her nose, pulling her hand away and rubbing her fingers together. "What is it?"

"That, is a very good question," he said, breathlessly. He opened his eyes and looked at her. "And no one seems to have the answer for it."

A "hmpf" noise was all she could manage as she watched the slimy substance slide between her fingers. "It's quite gross, whatever it is."

The Calling

"I'll not argue that one with you." He turned his head to the creek before looking back over at her. "Can you help me to the water?"

"Of course," she said, standing and reaching down to help him up. It was easier said than done, though. He was dead weight and she grunted with the effort to get his feet under him. By the time he was standing, his legs shook as he leaned against her and she was covered in slime. "Where do you usually change back?"

"Close to home," he said. "Or wherever my campsite is."

"You camp?" She looked up and watched him smile.

"It wouldn't be a great idea to run through Bluff's Point while in wolf form, now would it?"

"No," she said, before taking the first step with him toward the creek. "I guess that explains all the camping gear in your truck." They reached the creek bank and he nearly fell in face first as she tried to lower him back to the ground. He was sitting half in and half out of the water and she let go of him to remove her shoes and socks and roll her pants legs up. She stepped into the creek and gasped as the water hit her skin. "Shit this is cold."

Garrett leaned over, propping his weight up with one arm and reached out with the other to scoop a hand full of water up and splashing it on his face. Rayna bent her knees, washing her hands and arms free of the slime before walking to him and helping him wash. His skin was impossibly warm and slick and the more she rubbed her wet hands over him, and felt his muscles under her palms, the more she wanted to touch him. She pushed the thought away, helping him to wash away the remnants of the wolf. When his skin glowed, he looked up at her.

"I have spare clothes in the truck, behind the seat. Can you grab them for me?"

She smiled and walked out of the water, slipping her shoes back on before running back to the truck. She saw Jacob lying by the fire, his eyes closed. A quick search of Garrett's truck and she found several sets of clothes and an assortment of shoes. "His clothing bill must be outrageous," she said to herself as she grabbed a pair of jeans, a t-shirt, socks and boots.

When she made it back to where she'd left him, he was gone. "Garrett?"

"Over here."

She turned to the sound of his voice. He was hidden in the shadow of the trees, lying on the blanket she'd dropped earlier. Making her way to him, she sank to her knees beside him. "Are you all right?"

"Yeah," he said. "Just tired."

She reached out, brushing his wet hair away from his forehead. His eyes were closed, his breaths taken quickly as if he were winded. He looked up at her before raising his arm, taking her hand and kissing her palm. "Come here," he said, tugging her down to him.

Rayna lay down beside of him, molding her body against his. He sighed, his eyes once again closing before he nuzzled the side of her neck. His lips were warm as he brushed them against her skin and she realized then how hot his body was. He felt feverish. She touched his forehead, the side of his face and his chest, feeling the heat. "You're burning up, Garrett. Are you sure you're all right?"

The Calling

He nodded. "Hmm. My body temperature elevates in wolf form. It'll return to normal soon." She wasn't sure she believed him. She'd never felt anyone's skin so hot. He opened his eyes to look at her and smiled. "I'm fine, Rayna. I couldn't catch a cold if you sneezed in my face, let alone get sick from anything else. My metabolism and body temperature make it damn near impossible to be infected with anything. I'm already infected, remember?"

"You can't get sick?"

"No."

"Never?" He shook his head. "No flu bugs or stomach virus?"

"No."

"STD's?"

"What part of no aren't you getting?" he asked, laughing, pulling her body closer to him. "I can't get sick, ever, so stop worrying."

She grinned and ran her hand over his chest, fingering one nipple and smiling as it tightened. He made a small noise in the back of his throat before brushing her forehead with his lips. His hand slid down over her ribs, resting on her hip before sliding behind her to her bottom. He pulled her to him, pressing her into his body. She felt him then against her leg, thick and hard. "I thought you were tired," she said, smiling.

"Never too tired for you."

Rayna ran her hand down his stomach and glanced up at his face. He was watching her, his gaze penetrating. She leaned back enough to get her hand between them and he sucked in a harsh breath when her fingers skimmed the head of his cock.

His eyes fluttered closed as she wrapped her hand around him, fisting his hardened length in her palm. He moaned and threw his head back, his neck impossibly long. "Christ, Rayna, don't stop."

Eleven

Rayna stroked him from base to tip, watching his lips part before she leaned forward, burying her face against his throat. She sucked his flesh into her mouth, using her teeth on him lightly. His fingers wound in her hair, holding her head to him and she kissed her way to the side of his neck, up his jaw and across the stubble on his cheek. When he turned his head and opened his eyes, she smiled. "I take it you're feeling a little better."

He made a sound deep in his throat before his mouth covered hers, his tongue slipping past her lips. Desire burned through her limbs, tiny sparks of need firing off nerve endings that caused her body to ache. She worked her wrist, continuing to stroke him as his kiss became more aggressive. His hold on her tightened, his fingers in her hair pressing into her scalp. When he reached down and grabbed her wrist, he broke the kiss.

"Another minute of that and I'm done for," he said. "It's been too long."

She looked up at him through her lashes. "How long?"

He smiled. "Since you," he said. He pushed her hair away from her face, his fingertips brushing her cheek.

"I didn't leave you for someone else, Rayna. I left you to keep you safe. It's the hardest thing I've ever had to do."

"You could have told me."

"And then I would have lost you forever. I may not have been able to be with you after I broke things off but you were still there. If I had told you what I was…" He sighed. "I couldn't take the chance. I would have rather loved you from a distance than not have you near me at all."

Rayna's heart skipped a beat at his words. Did he just say he loved her? He kissed her cheek, the side of her mouth and chin before peppering kisses across her face. He didn't say another word and she knew then he didn't realize he'd said it. Did he mean it the way it sounded, though? Did he love her?

He kissed her again, his tongue slipping between her lips, licking and tasting. He kissed her until her body burned and throbbed with need, heat pooling between her legs. His hand slid under the back of her shirt, his fingers dancing along her spine until he reached her bra strap. With one flick of his fingers, the material parted.

"Let me see you," he said.

She leaned back, pushing to her knees and lifting her shirt over her head before slipping her bra off. He smiled and made a small noise in the back of his throat before lifting his hand, his fingers teasing her nipples. When he looked up at her, she could tell by the look on his face what he wanted. "We don't have any protection, Garrett, so don't go getting any ideas. You can play. That's all."

The smile widened. "Are you still on your birth control?"

"Yes."

"Then we're fine," he said, sitting up. He kissed the side of her neck, his fingers tormenting her nipples until her entire chest ached. "I can't catch anything, remember? No colds? No STD's?" He grinned as he palmed her breasts and looked up at her. "As long as your birth control is in order, we're fine."

"Then why did we always use condoms?"

He laughed. "You asked, so I wore them. It wasn't exactly something I could explain away, now was it?"

"No."

He lowered his head, nibbling her breasts before sucking a nipple into his mouth, his tongue flicking across it and shooting sparks straight to her core. "I know you want me, Rayna," he mumbled against her skin. "Take these jeans off. It's been months since I've had you."

She stood without hesitation and unfastened her jeans. He was propped up on one arm, watching her. The trees filtered the moonlight here but it was bright enough to cast him in silvery shadows. His gaze was intent on her, watching every move she made, and her pulse leaped as he raised his eyes to hers. No matter how awful he'd been to her in the past, she still wanted him. Had wanted him when he left her near tears and her heart aching for a kind word. The thought of those months made her pause as she stared down at him.

"What is it?" he asked.

Her shoulders drooped and her chest felt tight all of a sudden. She glanced away from him, staring at nothing, before looking back. "You're not going to decide I'm better off without you and chase me away again are you?

Because I don't think I can handle giving myself to you only to have you hurt me again when this is all over."

The look that crossed his face caused tears to burn the back of her eyes. "I'll never hurt you again," he said, softly. "And you'll have to beat me away with a stick to get rid of me." Rayna smiled. She could tell by the look on his face he meant it. When he tugged on the waistband of her jeans and helped her pull them down, she stepped out of them and sucked in a breath when he leaned forward, kissing her thigh before pulling her to stand between his upraised knees. His hands slid up the back of her legs, cupping her bottom as his mouth climbed higher. He nuzzled her through her panties, his breath hot against her.

He looked up at her before pulling the front of her underwear down enough to expose most of her to him. He lowered his head again, his tongue working into her folds and she moaned as her limbs jolted with fire. She helped him push her panties down and spread her legs for him, closing her eyes as his head went back between her thighs. He lapped at her, his tongue teasing her clit and she gasped when he sucked it into his mouth. Her fingers wound into his hair, holding him to her and a glance down at him was all it took for her body to ache with need. She moaned and threw her head back, her hips slanted toward him. A soft growl was heard moments before he wrapped his arm around her waist and pulled her forward. She yelped as they fell toward the blanket. She ended up on her hands and knees, straddling his face, and not once had he lost contact with her body.

Her eyes rolled and she gasped as his tongue entered her, his hold on her tightening as he fucked her with long, even strokes. Her arms shook and the desire to roll her hips was too much. She sat up on her knees, staring down at him and swallowed a gasp when she saw him staring up at her.

His eyes had bled to wolf amber.

She couldn't look away. Although it was Garrett under her she knew the wolf was there. Staring at her with those bright, alarming eyes. She watched him, seeing the creature she'd feared take her and her pulse raced faster. This was the beast that wanted her. Wanted to mark her as his, to claim her as his own, and as Garrett drove her half mad with his mouth, it was the wolf's penetrating stare that caused her body to shatter, to come undone under the knowledge that some tiny part of her wanted it too. She grabbed his head with both hands, threw her head back and bit her lip to keep from screaming, her hips moving against Garrett's face while he held her to him and sucked her clit into his mouth. Her body convulsed, her veins burning as every muscle blazed with her release.

When the last of the tremors faded, she leaned back, sitting on his chest and tried to catch her breath as Garrett peppered kisses across her thighs. The stars winked in and out of the tree limbs above her and she tried to focus on anything other than her pounding heart. When her breathing had returned to a more normal pace, she looked down.

The wolf was still there, watching her.

She smiled and slid down the length of Garrett's body, settling over him and impaled herself on his cock without a word. He moaned, his eyes closing briefly as he grabbed her. When he looked back up at her, she moved her hips and leaned down, brushing a kiss across his lips. "Has the wolf ever been in our bed?"

He licked her lips, his tongue darting into her mouth. "The wolf was always in our bed. I just never let you see him," he said. He grabbed her around the waist, lifting his hips to meet her downward strokes. "He wants you as much as I do."

There was nothing gentle about their lovemaking. Months of being denied each other erupted in hard, grinding movements. In hands and fingers grabbing the other hard enough to bruise. The wet sounds of undulating flesh and their harsh breaths pierced the silence of the forest. Rayna gave in to her desire and rode him until her legs trembled, until her lungs ached and every nerve in her body fired off sparks through her limbs. When she felt her stomach clench, her breath catching in her throat, she pressed her face to his neck, her nails digging into the blankets while she gasped out his name.

The world exploded in shards of bright light, her body shattering as she yelled and ground her hips into Garrett. His grunts increased, his hold on her tightening as he met each stroke with one powerful enough to force a sharp cry from her throat. His body jerked once, twice, before he climaxed, a throaty growl filling the air that sent goose bumps dancing along her limbs.

When he stilled, she could do nothing but lie there and try to catch her breath. He kissed the side of her face, his hand resting on the back of her head as he blew out a long breath, his chest rising and falling quickly under her. The minute she was able to talk she said, "Is it because it's been so long or was sex always that good before?"

The Calling

He chuckled and wrapped his arms tighter around her. "It was always that good for me." He kissed her cheek again, his lips brushing the side of her face before he paused. "Wait? Wasn't it always that good for you?"

She leaned up and smiled at him. "I don't know," she said. "It's been way too long for me to remember correctly. I may need more of a comparison. I can't base all sex on one act."

"The night is young," he said, "And lucky for you, I have the stamina of five men."

"Just five?" She squealed when he flipped her onto her back, his hips fitting between her parted thighs. He was still hard, she noticed, and smiled up at him. "Do you have the strength to prove that statement?"

He slid back inside her, the length of him filling her until their flesh met. "And then some," he said, leaning down to kiss her. "You'll be lucky to walk when I'm through with you."

"Can I shoot him now? I have a clear shot."

Caleb turned his head and scowled. "For the tenth time, no."

"What the hell are we waiting for," Bryce said, lowering the gun. "You said you wanted to watch and we did. Let's shoot him and get this over with."

"They're not finished," Caleb said, grinning.

"So we're just going to wait until he's through fucking her?"

Caleb leaned against the tree at his back and nodded his head. "Yes, that's exactly what we're going to do," he said. "Besides, you're the only one complaining." He turned his head, looking at the others. "The rest of you ready to call it a night?" A chorus of snickers and adamant rounds of "no," whispered along the pines. "There, see? No one wants to leave but you."

Bryce sat back down and propped his elbows on his knees, staring at the ground. "Man, I don't want to be out here all night."

"We'll be here for as long as it takes. Malcolm wants both of them. We can't even see Jacob from here but I know he's down there and I don't want him to get any heroic ideas. If the kid gets killed, the others will be harder to control. Besides, can't you give the man one last night with his girl? He'll be dead this time tomorrow. Now shut up before he realizes we're here." Caleb turned his attention back to Garrett and Rayna, smiling as he watched them. They'd been at it for over an hour and even though he'd settled his group of men high up on the rise, he could see enough to make him not want to disturb the scene below him. He could hear them even better as their voices carried through the clearing and that little brunette was a moaner. His dick throbbed every time he heard the breathy sounds she made. As much as he hated Garrett, he had to give the man credit. He wasn't letting his recent shift stop him from fucking his girl silly.

If Carmen could only see her favorite wolf now, he thought, grinning. She'd rip her own hair out. He should have brought a camera just so he could see the

The Calling

look on her face while he showed her what her beloved Garrett had been up to all night.

He wasn't stupid enough to think Carmen only had one agenda. He knew her better than she thought he did and he wasn't the brainless Alpha with a constant hard on she believed him to be. He knew who she really wanted and it wasn't him, regardless of what she said. It was Garrett she wanted, her Alpha. The man her wolf picked as her equal. No matter how many times she whored herself out in his bed, he knew what she wanted. She wanted a pawn to help her achieve her ultimate goal. To win Garrett and set herself up as mate to the pack leader. What the stupid bitch didn't realize was, Garrett didn't want her. He never did.

He smiled and settled back, his eyes boring into the two lovers at the bottom of the hill. If things went as he planned, then Carmen would spend the rest of her existence begging him for another day at life. He'd been her lapdog for more years than he wanted to remember and *his* reign was about to begin. Once Malcolm was out of the picture, he would kill Garrett and force Carmen, and Garrett's little bitch, to serve him and him alone. His smile widened as he thought of it and watched with renewed interest as the girl clawed at Garrett's back, her legs wrapping around his hips. He could hear her again, her small moans of pleasure like music to his ears and he wondered just how loud she could scream. He'd find out. He'd make her scream while Garrett watched.

Twelve

For the first time in eight months, Rayna woke wrapped in warmth. She smiled and buried her face against Garrett's chest, sighing when his arms tightened around her. He kissed the top of her head, his fingers sinking deeper into her hair. "We have to get up now, don't we?" He made a "Hmm," noise and slid his leg between her thighs but gave no other indication he was ready to move.

The sun was just barely peeking through the trees. She blinked at the lightening sky, barely holding back a smile as she remembered the previous night. Her body still ached as her abused muscles tried to recover from the strain she'd put on them. Garrett had made up for their eight-month separation like a man possessed. He took her to the edge of paradise and back again, never once letting her catch her breath in between. Her body had burned until she'd cried with the intensity of it. When she lay trembling under him, his lips and tongue tasting every inch of her flesh, she'd never felt more alive.

He raised his head all of a sudden and she felt his body go stiff against her. He pulled the blanket up, hiding her exposed backside and his arms tightened around her. "What is it?" He didn't say anything for long minutes and finally released the tight hold he had on her. Leaning back, he smiled down at her and kissed her lightly on the lips.

"Probably just Jacob," he said, "But I'm not taking any chances. Get dressed so we can get out of here."

She reluctantly untangled herself from him and gathered her clothes as he did the same. They dressed without a word and when he stood and reached down to help her off the ground, she saw Jacob standing by the truck. He was looking into the forest and she wondered if he sensed something. The same something Garrett had sensed.

They left the blanket and walked to where Jacob stood. He looked over at them when they approached. "I haven't seen or smelled anyone but I feel like I'm being watched. I've felt it all night."

"Then chances are, we have been," Garrett said, grabbing Rayna's arm and starting around the truck. "Let's get out of here."

Garrett didn't wait for Jacob to catch up. He started down the old trail he'd used to drive into the clearing and wondered if entering the forest wouldn't be a better choice. They wouldn't be out in the open but the trees were enough camouflage for the pack to hide, unseen, until they were ready to attack and Rayna wouldn't be able to escape through the trees as fast as Jacob could.

He gritted his teeth at his stupidity. He should have moved last night, taken her and ran as far as he could have. But no, he'd let his dick do the thinking. It was probably a mistake he would live to regret. He hadn't sensed anyone all night but that didn't mean they weren't there. He'd been too content to think of anything other than how Rayna had felt under him, how the small noises she made drove him half crazy and how badly he wanted to sink his teeth into her and make her his.

"Garrett, you're hurting me."

He looked down, noticing how white her face was and how tight he held her arm. He let go of her. "I'm sorry."

"It's all right," she said, rubbing her arm.

He looped his arm over her shoulder and leaned down, kissing the top of her head. "As soon as we get you out of here, I'm going to make all this shit up to you."

She grinned. "I don't know if you can ever make all this up to me, Garrett. The payment for treating me so bad alone is going to wear your ass out, not to mention dragging me into some turf war with your crazed wolf family."

He laughed and dropped his arm, grabbing her hand instead. "I can hardly wait," he said. "And I promise you, no matter what your demands, I can keep up."

"We'll see about that."

Jacob jogged in front of them and turned his head. "If we're where I think we are, there's a bend just up ahead. We're only a half a mile from Rusty's place. He has a clunker of a car but it runs. We might not make it to the county line but it'll be far enough from here that it won't matter."

Garrett nodded his head and walked faster. "Lead the way, then."

Jacob took off running, putting a great distance between them in a matter of seconds. Garrett looked down at Rayna and said, "Up for another run or do you want a lift?"

The Calling

"Depends on how fast you plan on running," she said, raising an eyebrow at him. "I'm only human, you know."

"Then a lift it is." He scooped her up into his arms without missing a step and took off before she even had a good hold of him. Her arms tightened around his neck as his feet ate up the path and he caught Jacob just as he darted from the road and into the forest.

"Is everything ready?" Malcolm asked.

Carmen smiled at him and walked across the room. "It's ready. It would take a miracle for him to get out of that."

"The collar will hold?"

"Yes," she said. "We won't have any surprises. Garrett will be utterly defenseless."

Malcolm looked down at her, taking in her red lips and the smile she was giving him. "I wouldn't underestimate his abilities, Carmen. I have no doubt what he'll do if he is freed."

"But he won't be free," she said. "He'll be caged like a dog. All he can do is watch."

"And that is another mistake. Making him watch will only push him further."

She ran her hand up his chest and leaned into him. "And the pack needs to see you in control of any situation. Once you've tamed the beast and destroyed him in front of them, their commitment to you will be reinforced. They want a powerful leader," she said. "And bringing Garrett down will show them who has the power. They fear him more than they fear you. They always have. Is that any way to lead? Show them the ruthless wolf I know is hiding under all this flesh and there isn't anything you can't get them to do."

Malcolm turned away from her and looked around the room. Everything seemed to be in order but he had a bad feeling. Something wasn't right and he wasn't sure what it was. *Probably the bitch at your back*, he thought, barely containing the growl clawing at his chest. He let his features slacken and turned back to face her. "Go see to our guests and make sure everything is ready. I want Ms. Ford completely relaxed before we begin." She walked away, her hips swaying with every step. Tonight would prove to be interesting no matter the outcome. The other Breed leaders were waiting for his show, he had a new wolf, and come this time tomorrow, he would have another, one that would be their salvation. All he had to do was keep Garrett's wolf from killing them all before he had a chance to see his plans fall into place.

Turning, he walked to the stairs, leaving the basement and heading to the upper rooms in the house. Caleb would return soon and he wanted to be there when his prize was returned to him.

"Do you ever get the feeling that no matter what you do, you just can't win?"

Garrett sat Rayna on her feet and stared down the hill toward Rusty's house. He saw the car Jacob had wanted to take. He also saw no less than ten people standing next to it, four of which he recognized as pack members. Were they waiting on them or was this just a coincidence?

"What do we do now?" Jacob asked.

"We'll, we obviously can't take the car," Garrett said.

"Why not?" Jacob grinned. "Surely you can take that many. It's only ten."

Garrett shot him a heated glance. "And six of them are humans."

"No, they're all pack," Jacob said.

He turned back to the men milling around the car. "I only recognize four. Where did the others come from?"

"Caleb has been recruiting."

Garrett's eyes widened. "What do you mean, recruiting?"

"Well, more like forced recruiting," he said. "There's a small group of them out by the old mine. Not sure why they don't associate with the pack much, but Malcolm knows they're there."

"And why is Caleb infecting people?"

Jacob shrugged his shoulder. "Building a private army?" he said. "Who knows? I haven't heard anything other than we have new pack members on a weekly basis now and Malcolm isn't happy about it."

Garrett crossed his arms over his chest and studied the men. If these were all Caleb's, then it made him wonder what Caleb was up to by infecting them all. There had to be a reason. No one just "made" a werewolf for the fun of it. Then again, this was Caleb. He always was impetuous. He'd get one crazy idea and run with it no matter how insane it seemed to anyone else and it was hard to tell how crazy he'd grown over the last twelve years.

Turning to look over his shoulder, he scanned the forest before glancing at Rayna. She was staring at the house, chewing on her bottom lip. Her eyes were slightly widened and he could taste just a hint of fear on her. He turned to Jacob. "Let's go back," he said. "We'll have to find another way. If these men belong to Caleb's group of recruits then its hard to tell what they're up to. I'd rather keep guessing than walk in there unprepared." Grabbing Rayna's hand he turned, leading her back into the forest. They hadn't taken four steps when a small popping noise, followed by a sharp whiz disturbed the air and echoed through the woods. Jacob yelled a moment later and Rayna squealed as Garrett grabbed her and threw her to the ground. The sound of Jacob's pained moans filled the air before all went deathly quiet.

"Stay down," Garrett said before jumping to his feet. She watched him run toward the trees and turned her head to look at Jacob. He was on the ground, his eyes closed, with an odd-looking metal dart sticking out of his back.

She heard the rustle of multiple feet running and leaned up, looking for Garrett. She saw him running toward her and was on her feet before he reached her. He grabbed her arm and pulled her through the trees, racing up the hill.

The sound of voices and laughs caused her heart to race out of control. Another shot from the gun whistled through the trees and she screamed. They were being hunted. Her eyes burned with unshed tears.

When they topped the hill, they both slid to a stop. Rayna panted for breath as she looked at the assembly of men waiting for them. She recognized Bryce and Caleb but the others she'd never seen before.

"Finally," Caleb said, his bright blue hair shining under the sun coming through the trees. "Do you have any idea how much sleep I've lost since you rolled into town, Garrett?"

Garrett's grip on her arm tightened before he took a step in front of her.

"Well, I'll tell you," Caleb said. "It took an entire day to heal that lucky shot you got in on me and I certainly didn't get much sleep that night." He lifted the hem of his shirt, showing the bright red, ragged scar slashing across his stomach. "Looks good though, don't it?" He dropped the shirt and looked back up. "Of course, the moment I could stand, Malcolm insisted on me chasing your worthless ass all over this mountain until I found you and we both know how that turned out, but I'm almost glad it was a stalemate otherwise I wouldn't have been rewarded the way I was. Catching you with your pants down, literally, was the highlight of my year. I lost sleep last night too." He grinned and said, "You know I had to watch. We all did."

The chorus of laughter that followed his comment made Rayna's stomach turn. They had been seen? These men watched while her and Garrett…

"Great show by the way, Garrett," Caleb said, grinning. "Who knew you could get a girl that worked up. Do you think she'll scream for me when I fuck her?" His leer was obscene and the moment he stuck his tongue out and wiggled it at her, Garrett jumped.

"Garrett!" Rayna screamed as Bryce lifted the gun. The sound it made as it went off caused her scream to echo long after Garrett hit the ground. She fell to her knees by his side, but was jerked up by her arm a moment later.

"Don't get too close, sweetheart," Caleb said, pulling her to him. "We want to make sure he's out incase he comes up fighting. I'd hate for him to hurt you."

Garrett didn't move. He was face down on the leafy forest floor and the tears she'd been fighting slid down her cheeks. When Bryce took a step toward Garrett's prone form and lifted the gun again, she barely managed to scream, "No!," before he shot him again. The same odd-looking dart that had been shot into Jacob stuck from Garrett's back. She wasn't sure what it was but as quick as he'd gone down, she assumed it was some sort of powerful tranquilizer.

Caleb stuck his foot out, placing it on Garrett's shoulder before giving him a couple of rough shoves. When Garrett didn't move, he motioned for Bryce, who bent to one knee and flipped him over. The first dart was in his neck.

"You almost missed him," Caleb said. "What the hell would you have done if you had, besides bleed to death, when he gutted you?"

Bryce looked up, anger shining in his eyes. "It wasn't me he was coming after, Caleb. It was you and your big mouth."

The Calling

Caleb snorted a laugh and held Rayna's arm tighter. "Take him back to the main house. Leave the kid. We have no use for him. I'll bring the girl."

"She can ride with this one," Bryce said, standing.

"She could," Caleb said, turning to look at her. "But I'd rather take her myself." His smile was lewd and a chill ran up her spine when he raked his gaze over her body.

Her stomach twisted into a tight knot and she tried to take a step back away from him but his hold on her arm tightened. She couldn't have spoken if she needed to. It was apparent to her something was going on that she probably didn't want to know about. She had a bad feeling and her stomach turned at the thoughts running through her head.

"She goes with this one, Caleb."

Caleb took a step toward Bryce and she saw his eyes bleed from pale blue to wolf amber. He growled, the sound dull and threatening and Rayna held her breath as her pulse raced. "Since when do you give the orders, Bryce? I'm second in command. You do as I say!"

"You may be Malcolm's second, but I don't think he'll be too pleased with what you're planning."

"And how do you know what I'm planning?"

Bryce made a small, "Hmpf," noise before lifting the gun slightly. "I'm not stupid, Caleb. We all know the only reason you made us sit all night and watch those two was for your own sick reasons and I also know why you want the girl alone. Now take her to the truck or I swear, I'll shoot you and leave you out here. I don't think Malcolm will be pissed when he finds out why."

The rumbling growl grew louder and Rayna could tell by the look on Caleb's face he didn't like being ordered around, especially by Bryce. His fingers tightened around her arm, the sting causing a small whimper to escape her throat, and it was enough for Bryce to lift the gun and point it at Caleb.

"Either walk her to the truck or let her go."

Caleb stared at Bryce for long minutes and Rayna was sure Bryce would have to fire that gun. She wanted him to if Caleb's plan for her was what she thought it was. Getting raped by some sex-starved werewolf while Garrett was unconscious and unable to help her caused the bile in her stomach to rise. The fear she'd felt when topping the hill and seeing these men multiplied ten-fold as the minutes slowly ticked by. When Caleb finally let go of her, she sighed in relief and fought the urge to run to Bryce's side. He was still one of the bad guys in her book but at least she knew he was trying to protect her to some extent.

The other men finally walked forward and lifted Garrett from the ground. She watched them, her chest aching as they none to gently carried him down the hill. When she looked at Bryce and he motioned her forward, she gave one last glance at Caleb. His gaze was on her, those bright amber eyes burning into her. She turned and followed the others, hoping this nightmare would soon be over.

Thirteen

Much to her surprise, once they reached Malcolm's house, Rayna had been led to her room and told to shower and change. That was over two hours ago. There was constant commotion in the house. She could hear voices and smell food and as much as she wanted to get out of there, find Garrett and Mitch and run, it was useless. They'd locked her in and nothing she did would budge the door.

The room looked exactly as it had the last time she was in it and the gun she'd packed into the inner pocket of her suitcase was still there. She'd dressed in jeans and a loose fitting button-up silk blouse and left it to hang over her pants. The gun was tucked into the waistband of her jeans at the small of her back. If she were lucky, no one would find it. If she weren't, their chances of getting out of there were dwindling by the second. She had no idea where they had taken Garrett. Not in the house, she was sure. If he was, then Malcolm was an idiot. Surely he knew Garrett wouldn't let them hurt her.

The thought of that made her stomach cramp. Malcolm wanted to infect her. To turn her into a werewolf. Her sudden burst of laughter at the idea echoed off the walls. Two days ago she hadn't believed in the existence of werewolves. She believed in them now. She had a two-hundred-pound furry boyfriend to prove they existed. And now it looked like she was going to be joining the tall, dark and scary club. The fear alone left her numb. Malcolm had said the bite would only hurt for a minute. But what about after that? What happened to the body once infected? When her bones started to shift and changed? How much pain would that be? According to Jacob, a lot.

Voices in the hall caught her attention and she leaned back against the wall and listened. It was Malcolm and whomever he was talking to was getting an ear full. He didn't sound happy.

The doorknob jiggled before she heard the tumbler inside the lock turn. Malcolm opened the door. He was dressed in a suit that looked expensive, his hair was neatly combed and even though she hated to admit it, he looked quite nice.

"Ms. Ford," he said, smiling. "I'm glad to see you safe and sound."

"I wouldn't exactly call me safe. I'm being held against my will."

"Everything will be fine, I assure you." He pushed the door open wide and continued to smile at her. "I have a meal prepared for us. If you would like to join me?"

She wanted to refuse but the very mention of food caused her stomach to growl. She hadn't eaten since the dry rabbit the day before. Pushing away from the wall, she pulled her shirt down, concealing the gun, and walked to where he stood. "After you," she said.

The Calling

"Nonsense," Malcolm said, bending his arm and offering it to her in a gentlemanly fashion. "I would be honored to escort you."

She rolled her eyes at him, ignoring his offered arm, and walked past him into the hall. Bryce was there, leaning against the opposite wall. His gaze was averted but she saw him glance up at her as she passed him.

The bottom floor of the house was packed with people, or more specifically, werewolves. She had no doubt they were. They looked human enough but after everything she'd seen, she knew better. She looked at the faces of everyone she passed trying to see if she recognized any of them. Judith was the only one that looked familiar to her.

A hand suddenly landing on her back caused her to nearly jump out of her skin. She whirled around to see Malcolm's startled face and she took a deep breath before letting it out.

"I didn't mean to frighten you," he said. "I merely wanted to direct you to the dining room."

She took a step back, keeping her eye on those standing in the foyer. "Then point the way. You don't have to touch me to do that."

"Very well. Right this way."

He motioned toward the hall and she stared at the faces of those she passed. She didn't know why they were all there. Unless they came to watch the big girl pee her pants when some hairy, slobbering werewolf attacked her.

The dinning room held another group of people. These looked much more important than the ones in the hall. Their clothing alone told her that and smiles lit their faces when she entered the room.

They were dressed as nicely as Malcolm was, some better. The men's suits appeared to be tailored and the few women in the room looked ready for a grand ball. Evening gowns that sparkled under the lights made her feel way under dressed.

A table large enough to seat twenty people took up the center of the room. Fine china in white and gold was placed on a tablecloth of blood red. Crystal goblets sparkled under a multitude of candles that sat in ornate candelabras scattered around the room. The lighting was subdued and, if she only admitted it to herself, made everything look very elegant. Malcolm may be an evil werewolf but he sure knew how to throw a party.

Malcolm stopped beside her and she took a step to the side, putting distance between them. "Ms. Ford," he said. "I'd like for you to meet our guest. Most of them have traveled a great distance to meet you."

"I don't want to meet your friends, Malcolm."

"I'm sure you will be most intrigued," he said. He took her arm, just above the elbow and she wanted to pull from his grasp. The multitude of curious gazes stopped her from doing so.

The people in the room watched her curiously as Malcolm led her toward the front of the room. When he stopped, she gritted her teeth as she stared at everyone looking back at her.

"My friends," Malcolm said, "Welcome. I'm sorry for the delay but we had a few problems in our plan that we didn't foresee but all is well now." He released her arm and smiled. "I'd like to introduce Ms. Rayna Ford. She's the woman we've chosen to handle our transition into the world. She was quite skeptical at first but I'm sure she'll be more inclined to accept the rest of what we have to show her."

A man toward the back of the room walked forward and Rayna raised one eyebrow at him. He was tall, strongly built with wide shoulders and his hair was as black as Carmen's. His suit was light gray, the coat left unbuttoned. His shirt was black and the way the light shined against it, she assumed it was silk. He was quite attractive, had the most intense green eyes she'd ever seen but one look at him told you he didn't like the outdoors. His flesh was the palest shade she'd ever seen. The sunlight hadn't hit this man in ages.

He stopped just short of her and, never breaking eye contact with her, bowed his head slightly. "Ms. Ford," he said. "It's a pleasure to meet you. I'm Sabriel."

Malcolm took a slight step forward, just enough for her to see his face. He turned his head toward her and smiled. "Sabriel has traveled half the globe to join us this evening. He too is eager for our venture to succeed."

"And what venture is that?" Rayna asked.

Sabriel nodded his head and glanced at Malcolm. "To see our kind brought into the public light."

"You're kind?" She tilted her head slightly. "You're a werewolf also?"

He smiled and when he did, Rayna gasped when she saw his teeth. "No," he said. "I'm not a shifter. I'm a Vampire."

Two perfectly sharp canines glistened as he smiled and as hard as she tried, she couldn't stop staring. She glanced up, met his eyes briefly and looked back at his teeth…. and laughed. She laughed until his smile faltered. He looked stunned and glanced at Malcolm before turning his attention back to her. Regardless of what was happening to her, Rayna wasn't completely rude. She stifled the laugh and cleared her throat. "I'm sorry," she said. "You just caught me a bit off guard."

Sabriel glanced at Malcolm, his eyes narrowing. "I thought you explained to her what it is we all want? Or have you deceived us all? The benefits of this venture were to all breeds, not just the wolves."

"And as I told everyone, Sabriel, there were complications. The discussion of exactly whom it was she would be helping didn't quite happen."

Sabriel turned his attention back to her. "Exactly what were you told, Ms. Ford?"

"That werewolves existed and they wanted to go public."

He straightened and threw a glance at Malcolm. The whispers in the room grew then. "Werewolves aren't the only breeds, Ms. Ford. We are many in number. I represent the vampires and the others you see here are representatives of their breed. There are many who do not wish to be known but, like the wolves, some of us grow tired of hiding. The shifters number in the thousands and only a small portion of the breeds are present."

"What do you mean by breeds?" she asked. He turned his head and peered at the room and as every person present slowly made their way to her and introduced themselves, her world expanded just a little bit more. Learning werewolves existed had shaken her to the core. Meeting a vampire, fangs and all, had startled her, but after the shock Malcolm had given her when she arrived, Sabriel's announcement seemed like trivial information. But now, as she stared up at the human faces that greeted her and learned that not only did werewolves exist but also werelions, weretigers, and werelepards, her world grew to astronomical proportions. She shook her head and grinned. "So, we have lions and tigers and... leopards? I thought it would be bears."

"The bears couldn't make it."

Rayna shot a look to Sabriel when he spoke and laughed until her stomach ached. "Please tell me you're joking." That fanged smile greeted her again and his face lit up. She'd thought him attractive before but the mirth shining in his eyes made him damn near beautiful. Her pulse raced just a little bit faster as she stared at him and she found it hard to look away. His gaze roamed her features, down the line of her body, and her skin felt warmed with his brief glance, as if he'd touched her flesh with that fleeting look. A small shiver raced up her spine, her stomach clenching delightfully and she shook her head, looking away from him. The sensation left as quickly as it came when she did.

"As I said," Sabriel added, "only a small portion of breeds are represented this evening."

"I see." Rayna looked at everyone, ignoring Sabriel's gaze, as they continued to stare at her and movement at the back of the room caught her attention. Her eyes widened moments later when she saw who was standing in the far corner. "Mitch!" She pushed past Sabriel and the others and ran to him, sliding to a stop when he shrank back from her. She stared at him, watching him turn his face toward the wall. "Mitch?" When he did nothing but ignore her, she took a small step closer. "Are you all right?" she asked. She touched his arm and he pulled away.

"Don't touch me, Rayna."

She closed the remaining distance between them. "Mitch," she whispered. "I've been worried about you. Are you all right?"

He laughed. "Define all right?"

Turning his head, he looked at her and Rayna noticed his bloodshot eyes. His skin looked pale and she'd never seen him look so distraught. "What did they do to you?"

"What didn't they do?" he said, glancing across the room. She looked over her shoulder, noticing the others watching them and turned back to Mitch and whispered, "Garrett is here. He's going to get us out."

"Garrett?" he said. "As in Kincaid?" At her nod, he added, "What the hell is he doing here?"

"Long story," she said. "But he'll come get us."

"Where is he now?"

Sleeping off the tranquilizer, probably. "He'll be here soon," she said, hoping she was correct and fearing she wasn't. "The boy Jacob was trying to help me escape as well. As soon as they get here, we'll go home."

He shook his head, his eyes filling with tears. "I can't go home, Rayna. Not after what they've done to me. They turned me into a monster."

Her heart ached as she watched him and gripped his arm in her hand. "Everything will be okay. I promise."

"Nothing will ever be okay. Not now." Mitch looked over her shoulder and she turned, seeing Malcolm at the head of the table. He was watching her. When he smiled and straightened, she knew he wanted her attention.

The Calling

"Ms. Ford. Mr. Pierson. If you both would like to join us."

"Actually I wouldn't," Rayna said.

His smile remained as soft murmurs whispered across the room. "Please, join us," he said. "Our meal is getting cold."

The people in the room started taking their seats, leaving the two beside Malcolm empty. She assumed those were their assigned seats. When the last person sat and Malcolm continued to stare at her, she sighed and turned back to Mitch. "Let's go get this over with." She took his hand and led him to the table, letting go of him to take her seat. Once they were seated, Malcolm looked down the table.

"My friends, again, I welcome you. Our delay was most unpleasant but the day we've all been waiting on is here. Please join me in a toast to Ms. Ford and Mr. Pierson." Everyone raised their glasses. "To our future," he said. "May it be as bright as we've all dreamed."

Rayna stared as they all lifted their glasses in her direction and she barely contained the urge the toss her wine glass at them. It would have been childish and regardless of what Malcolm had planned, she wouldn't loose her cool in front of these people no matter how much she wanted to. She'd had just about enough of being scared. With what they had planned, what was the worse they could do to her? Kill her? If Malcolm wanted her to shift in front of the media, that would happen anyway. Why prolong the inevitable?

When everyone settled and Malcolm took his seat, the murmur of voices slowly filled the room. The food was carried in and she raised an eyebrow at the fact Malcolm had "servants." Roast beef and steamed vegetables, thick sauces and fresh rolls that still looked warm caused her stomach to growl embarrassingly loud. She hoped no one noticed.

When the food was served and Malcolm took the first bite, the others followed. Her and Mitch just sat staring at their plates.

"Do you not find your meal acceptable?" Malcolm said. "I can have the cook prepare you something else if you'd like."

"It's not the food," she said. "It's what may be in it that concerns me."

He stared at her with a blank look on his face before he laughed. "I can assure you, Ms. Ford, poisoning you isn't my intention. You're very important to us."

"Drugs then?" she asked.

"No. No drugs. It's perfectly safe."

She glanced up at Mitch. He was watching her. Would they really drug her? Did she really care? If she were half out of her mind, wouldn't that be better than being fully aware? Especially if some big, hairy werewolf was going to take a little bite out of her. Picking up her fork, she started to eat.

After the first bite, the man seated next to her, one of the werelions if she remembered correctly, leaned toward her and said, "You'll be lauded as a hero among our people, Ms. Ford. We're very grateful for what you're doing."

Laying her fork down, she chewed the food in her mouth before turning to look at him. "What I'm doing is being forced into accepting something I don't want. Or is that how all of you are made? Some werewolf or werelion gets hungry and takes a small bite out of the guy sitting next to him on the bus and 'Ops!' another member of the furry club?" His cheeks reddened slightly before he glanced up at Malcolm.

"Most of the time it is accidental," Malcolm said, "But there are some that do choose to join us. Bryce is one of those. He came to us and requested the infection."

"And why is that?" she asked. "I can't see one benefit of becoming a werewolf."

"Well, the guarantee of a long life is one, not to mention the sense of power one gains."

She shrugged her shoulders. "Living forever can't be all it's cracked up to be and you know what power does to people, don't you? It distorts the mind and creates monsters. In your case, bigger monsters."

"Is that how you see us?" the woman sitting next to Mitch asked. She was brunette, her hair pulled into a complicated twist at the back of her head. She was pretty, looked to be in her forties, and still had the body of someone in their early twenties. Rayna couldn't remember what breed she was. "You think we're monsters?"

"Aren't you?" Rayna asked. "You force this infection on people and then expect them to thank you after it's all said and done. You might look harmless in your fancy dress and expensive hair-do but you're still a monster."

"Ms. Ford," Malcolm said. "Does Garrett know you look at us as monsters?"

She turned her head and shot him a glare that did nothing but cause him to smile. "What I feel for Garrett has nothing to do with you."

"Ah, I see," he said, smiling. "Since Garrett was attacked instead of asking for this gift, he is excluded from your disdain."

"Garrett isn't using his strength to hurt people. He isn't forcing this affliction on innocent humans. He lives his life in the real world and to my knowledge hasn't had any of the problems you seem to think will exist if you yourself venture off this mountain. So to answer your question, yes. I do exclude him from the monsters. He might go all furry but he doesn't hurt people just because he can."

The murmur of voices increased in volume and the smile on Malcolm's face looked damn near serene. He stared at her for long moments before looking down the table. "What did I tell you," he said. "Is she perfect or is she not?"

A chorus of cheers and clanking glasses followed. Rayna stared at them all as if they'd just grown another head. What the hell were they so damned happy about? She was trying to tell them off, not congratulating them. Malcolm turned his attention back to her, his smile still present as he gestured to her plate. "Eat, Ms. Ford. The night will be long and holds many surprises. You'll need your strength for what's to come."

Fourteen

Garrett was dreaming. He was warm and soft hands caressed his skin until he felt drugged from every small touch. A flutter of kisses brushed his face, the wet slide of a tongue was felt against his lips and he didn't fight the probing kiss that followed. A barely there sweep of long fingers tickled his stomach before his jeans were unfastened and the warmth of a hand enveloped his cock. He moaned into the kiss, lifting his hips as he was stroked and he tried to lift his hands. His arms felt like weights held them down and he tried to get closer to no avail. The kiss intensified, the warm body leaning against him was soft and lush and the fingers in his hair held his head still while he was kissed near breathless. He gasped, breaking the kiss and those soft lips closed over his nipple, biting gently and he nearly came. "Christ, Rayna, don't stop."

A feminine chuckle was heard and he realized then, he wasn't dreaming. The hand pumping his cock tightened as that wicked tongue on his nipple flicked the small puckered bud until he was panting and squirming. She licked a trail down his chest, kissing his stomach before licking the head of his cock. He forced his eyes open to watch her and froze.

"Hello lover," Carmen said, grinning before sucking him into her mouth.

Garrett jumped, trying to throw her off only to realize why his arms felt so heavy. They were chained to the wall above his head. A metal collar of some kind was around his neck and it too was held to the wall by a chain. Carmen laughed around his dick as he struggled and the sound vibrated straight to his balls. His vision bled to red as he bucked to try and get her off of him. When she released him and licked the length of him before sitting up, he grabbed the chains and used them as leverage as he leaned to one side and raised his knee, smashing it into the side of her head. Her shocked scream echoed off the walls as she flew across the room, landing with a hard smack against the opposite wall.

She lay motionless for long moments before she finally raised her head. Her lips curved into a smile before she climbed to her feet and pulled her skirt down. Nothing about her had changed in the twelve years since he'd left. She still wrapped her body in skin-tight material, which exaggerated her curves. The dress she wore was low cut, her breasts nearly spilling from the top and the skirt was short enough you didn't need to use your imagination to wonder if she was wearing panties. One glance and he knew. She wasn't.

The click of her heels echoed off the walls as she walked back across the room and he glanced at the chains that held him. He was sitting down and, using the links of metal for support, climbed wearily to his feet. He staggered when his head began to spin and sagged against the wall. When Carmen's feet came into his line of sight, he looked up.

The Calling

"You still taste good, Garrett."

"Fuck you, Carmen."

Her eyes widened and glistened in the low light. "Oh, it would be my pleasure, lover."

"I'm not your lover." He tested the strength of the chains as she stood there grinning at him. They were barely a foot in length and didn't give him much room to move. He also couldn't budge them from the wall. They were welded into metal hooks and looked solid. "And you come near me again," he said, "and you won't ever have another."

She laughed and stepped closer. "Don't tell me you didn't enjoy it, Garrett," she said, glancing down at his cock jutting from the front of his pants. "That beautiful little hard-on you have proves you did."

"I'm a man, Carmen. Your eighty-year-old grandmother could suck my dick and get the same reaction. Don't flatter yourself."

Her face reddened, her lips closing into a tight, white line before she closed the distance between them, standing just far enough away he couldn't reach her. "Don't lie to yourself, Garrett, and don't lie to me. I know you, remember? I've tasted every square inch of you and I know how to make you scream." She smiled again and raised her hands, pulling down the top of her dress. Her breasts spilled out and he kept his gaze locked on her face. "I still bear the marks of your love for me." She fingered the scars over her left breast. Five long slash marks that he himself had put there the first time he was stupid enough to crawl into her bed. Little did he know by letting the beast out and marking her would make her think he wanted her forever. "I know how much you want me, Garrett. How can you deny what we have?"

"Had," he said, straightening. "Past tense. And what we had was sex. Nothing more. I left Wolf's Creek, and you, for a reason, Carmen, and believe me when I say I haven't regretted it a day since."

She stared at him for long minutes before righting her clothes and smoothing her skirt down over her hips. "You prefer her over me?"

He wanted to laugh but figured it would only make her crazier. Did she honestly want him to answer that? He stared at her instead and wondered where they were keeping Rayna. The fact he hadn't thought of her before now weighed heavily on his mind. She should have been the first thing he thought of when waking. She was, he thought, his mind going back to the feelings that woke him. *You thought Rayna was sucking you off, not this bitch.* Pushing the sudden guilt away he focused his attention back on Carmen. She was watching him, her gaze locked firmly with his.

"You didn't answer my question," she said.

"You're not going to like the answer."

Her face reddened again. "She's nothing, Garrett. She's fragile and weak and can't possibly please you the way I can."

"That's where you're wrong," he said. "She pleases me more than you ever did."

She growled and stalked toward him and he used her stupid mistake to his advantage. The moment she was within touching distance, he reached out, grabbing two hands full of her hair and jerked her to him. Her startled gasp sounded like music to his ears and he pulled the strands of long black hair fisted between his fingers harder. "I could snap your conniving neck with one quick jerk," he said. "Give me one good reason not to." The fear he saw in her eyes caused a smile to lift the corner of his mouth. She stared up at him and swallowed audibly before shifting her weight on her feet.

"You kill me now, Garrett, and your girl is as good as dead."

"The first person who touches her will be dead before she finishes screaming whether you're alive to see it or not."

Carmen grinned at him before chuckling. "I hate to break it to you, lover, but you won't be able to do anything but watch." She raised her hand and touched his neck, fingering his skin above the metal collar. "You'll have no choice wearing this," she said. "It isn't too tight is it?" A lone finger slid between the metal and his skin and he realized then how tight it actually was. The ring felt thick and lay against his collarbone and ran halfway up his neck. He turned his head and felt the first pinch of something sharp. Carmen's smile told him whatever it was, wasn't put there by accident.

"This pretty little collar you have on won't exactly go with your fur coat," she said, "So I wouldn't suggest bringing that wolf to our party. The minute you try to shift, the collar will expand, exposing the metal studs imbedded inside the ring. By the time your wolf is out, your head will be ready to fall off those gorgeous wide shoulders of yours. What good will you do her then?"

He grabbed her chin, tilting her head up, and the thoughts running through his head caused his fingers to tighten, the one still in her hair twisting the strands until he felt them start to break from her scalp. The hand cupping her chin tightened, squeezing until his fingers were digging into the side of her face. Her pained gasp only fueled his rage and the wolf slid under his skin, trying to free himself. The bones in his face shifted, his claws extended and the first drop of blood that rolled down Carmen's cheek caused his bloodlust to rise, his fingers digging deeper. The wolf was coming, he felt it roll beneath his skin and just as Carmen said, the collar expanded as his neck grew thicker, the small metal spikes piercing his skin.

Clamping his teeth together, he closed his eyes and held the wolf back. He heard the roar inside his head and felt the tug of war as bone and skin started to shift then recede. When the noise inside his head finally calmed, he opened his eyes.

Malcolm was standing behind Carmen. "Let her go, Garrett."

He stared at him, his fingers tightening on Carmen's head. "Why should I?"

"Because I asked you to."

Garrett snorted a laugh. "Wrong answer."

"I need her," he said. "And so do you whether you choose to believe it or not."

"I don't need anything from any of you and the minute I get this contraption off, I'm going to prove it."

Malcolm smiled and nodded his head. "Point taken. Although, I would like to talk to you, alone, so if you wouldn't mind releasing her for now, I promise you'll get another chance to kill her. We both know she won't stay away from you. It's only a matter of time before she'll be back."

The Calling

Garrett looked down at her, watching her blood seep between his fingers. Her eyes were glassy, her lips void of all color. He wanted to kill her. Wanted to hear the crack of grating bones as he twisted her head and felt her neck break.

"Please, Garrett. Just postpone your vengeance for a little while longer."

He slung her away, watching her slide across the floor. She coughed and doubled over, trying to catch her breath. When she slowly climbed to her feet and pulled her skirt down over her hips, he wiped his bloody hand on his shirt and fastened his pants.

"Carmen," Malcolm said, "Go upstairs and find Caleb. We'll be ready to start soon."

She started across the room, her gaze locked on Garrett. "You'll be sorry for that, Garrett." Her eyes were bright amber and her soft growls filled the basement.

When she climbed the steps and was disappeared from view, Garrett leaned back against the wall and crossed his arms over his chest. "All right, old man. You have my attention. What do you want?"

When Carmen entered the sitting room, Rayna gasped. Carmen's normally pristine appearance was disheveled. Her hair looked as if she hadn't brushed it all day, her dress revealed more than she ever wanted to see but it was the condition of her face that shocked her. Blood ran in rivulets down the left side of her face, over her jaw and into the top of her dress. Holes were seen in her cheek and judging the distance between them, they looked suspiciously like someone had dug their fingers into her face.

The noise in the room died as she continued to cross the floor. Her steps were shaky but the look in her eyes caused Rayna to sit up straight in her chair. It only took seconds for her to realize those hate filled eyes were looking at her. When Carmen continued to advance, Rayna stood, backing up until her legs hit the chair.

Carmen raised her arm and as she neared her, swung her fist. Rayna's eyes widened seconds before it connected with her jaw. The bright, blinding light she saw only lasted a second as she flew backwards over the chair and landed in a heap on the floor.

The chaos that ensued was barely heard as she blinked and tried to focus her vision. Spots flew past her line of sight and the world darkened momentarily. Mitch's concerned voice snapped her back to reality and Carmen's wild, screeching voice was heard over the shouting in the room.

"Rayna? Can you hear me?"

Her ears were ringing and try as she might, she couldn't seem to focus her eyes on anything. Her vision blurred again and her eyes grew heavy. Something cold touched her cheek, the cool sensation washing through her body like ice water poured into her veins. She gasped and looked up. Sabriel was kneeling at her side.

"Are you all right?" he asked, concern etched into the set of his jaw and the look in his eyes.

She stared at him, noticing then his hand was on her face. The cooling sensation was still there. When he smiled at her and removed his hand, the feeling vanished.

The Calling

She blinked up at him and tried to smile. She wasn't sure she succeeded. Her jaw felt like someone had hit her with a two-by-four.

"Can you talk?" Mitch said. "Your jaw isn't broke is it?" He opened her mouth and she moaned. The pain brought tears to her eyes. "You still have all your teeth. Well, unless they fall out when you stand up." He grinned at her and she saw the old Mitch in the look he gave her. She rolled her eyes at him.

"It's not broke," she mumbled. "I don't guess it is."

"You're talking so that's a good sign. Can you sit up?" He grabbed her arm, Sabriel grabbing the other, and they helped her sit up. She saw Carmen immediately. The woman was on the other side of the room, pinned against the wall. Her hot gaze was focused on her and like the old saying goes, "If looks could kill," Rayna knew she'd be dead right about now. Why, she didn't know.

She saw Bryce walk across the room. He glanced down at her, a sympathetic look on his face before he looked at Sabriel. "Malcolm isn't back yet. What should we do with Carmen?"

"What would I do personally?" Sabriel said, "I would kill her but she isn't one of mine. Secure her until Malcolm returns."

When Bryce turned and motioned for the men holding Carmen to follow him, Carmen dug her heels into the carpet. "I bear his mark," she yelled, glaring at her from across the room. "It may be you who shares his bed but I'm the one his wolf has chosen. I'm his chosen mate!" She screamed as they yanked her out of the room and Rayna stared after her, letting her words rattle through her head. She was his mate? Was she talking about Garrett? Had Garrett claimed Carmen when he lived among these wolves? If so, then why did he say the wolf wanted her?

"You should sit," Sabriel said, his words drawing her from her thoughts. She looked up at him, the intense look on his face washing everything away. She couldn't explain what it was when he looked at her. It was as if everything around her calmed. The problems she faced seemed mundane and a lethargic peace settled into her bones. She wasn't sure if it was him or some fancy vampire mojo. She still remembered the cooling sensation his hand left on her face. He had a firm grip on her arm and she didn't feel it. Whatever he'd done, he wasn't doing it now.

He motioned her back to her chair, helping her cross the short distance, and when she finally sat and the ringing inside her head had stopped, the only thing she could think of was where they were keeping Garrett and why Carmen's hysterical words left her feeling so cold.

Malcolm grabbed a chair, sliding it forward. He sat, propped one ankle on the opposite knee and finally looked up. "What I want is simple, Garrett," he said. "I want you to join us."

Garrett laughed and shook his head. "Not going to happen."

"We're not the monsters you think we are, Garrett."

"You aren't doing much to disprove my theory, either."

"What if I see to it that you're the one to infect Ms. Ford?" Malcolm said. "I'm sure you would rather not let Caleb do it. He seems a little... eager. I'm afraid he may hurt the girl."

"No one will be infecting her. As soon as I get out of these chains..."

"You'll whisk her to parts unknown?" Malcolm laughed and stood from his chair, straightening his suit jacket before crossing the room and stopping in front of him. "Please, Garrett. Don't fool yourself into thinking you can keep her safe. We'll find her no matter where she is. Just play along and all will be well."

Footsteps on the stairs drew their attention and Garrett turned his head, watching Bryce enter the basement. "There are problems upstairs that need your immediate attention, Malcolm."

"What sort of problems?" Malcolm said.

Bryce glanced at Garrett before clearing his throat. "Carmen."

Malcolm sighed before turning back to Garrett. "Very well. Take our guest here to the clearing and secure him. I want to make sure he has a front row seat for our little show."

Garrett pulled on his chains, extending them as far as he could go. "I'll not let you hurt her, Malcolm."

"Then join us and see to her safety," Malcolm said. "I would hate to have to destroy you and leave her defenseless before the pack. We both know how the Alpha's get when there's a new female amongst us. Do you think she would survive the hunt when they all tried to claim her?" He smiled and turned, walking back to the stairs. "Think about it, Garrett. If you're not here to protect her, who will?"

Garrett watched him leave before turning his gaze to Bryce. He looked much like he did when he left twelve years ago. He was still tall, solidly built and had a face that could hide every thought he had. They stared at each other for long moments before Bryce finally moved.

"You do know I'll kill you the minute you take these chains off, right?"

Bryce smiled. "No you won't."

"And what makes you think that?"

"Because you'll have a reason not to."

"And that would be?" Garrett asked.

The smile Bryce gave him told him things words couldn't. Garrett stood stock still as he approached and watched him until he stopped in front of him. "Things are about to get real interesting around here, Garrett, and I for one can't wait for the fireworks."

Fifteen

When Malcolm returned, Rayna could tell by the look on his face he'd been told of the excitement he'd missed. He hurried across the room and knelt by her chair. "Are you all right, Ms. Ford?"

Rayna looked at him, her jaw aching and the side of her face feeling as if it would explode any minute, and said, "Actually, I'm having a wonderful time, Malcolm. Who knew a bunch of crabby old wereanimals could throw such an exciting party." He looked shocked for a moment before he offered her a tiny smile.

"Your sarcasm is well noted," he said. "I do apologize. Carmen will be dealt with."

She looked away, noticing everyone staring at her and leaned back in her seat. She closed her eyes and willed the headache pounding in her head away. "I want to see Garrett," she said, keeping her eyes closed.

"I'm afraid that isn't possible."

The look she shot him caused him to lean back. She stared at him and felt a bubble of hysterics try to surface. The only person she felt safe around was being kept from her and she was sick of all the games. She was sick of these people. Sick of playing by their rules and completely sick of being the victim. The gun was poking into her spine and in that moment, she felt brave enough to use it. "Then I'm afraid you give me no choice," she said, sitting up before reaching behind her back and grabbing the gun. She stuck the barrel just under his left eye and pushed until the skin around the black metal turned white. "Unless you have some fancy werewolf power that will allow you to grow a new brain, I suggest you take me to him now."

There wasn't a sound in the room. The silence was damn near deafening. Rayna kept her gaze locked with Malcolm and swallowed the fear trying to claw its way up her chest. She had no doubt he could take the gun if he wanted to. She just hoped she had enough nerve to pull the trigger if he tried.

He said nothing for long minutes, his gaze never leaving her own and she knew the moment he'd made a decision. A spark of something flashed in his eyes and he blinked at her before saying, "All right, Ms. Ford. As you wish." He stood and she followed him, keeping the gun pressed into his face. They stood awkwardly staring at each other before he motioned to the door with his arm. "After you."

"No," she said. "After you. I insist."

Malcolm turned and she turned with him, moving the gun to the side of his head, pressing it into his temple. They walked out of the room and down the hall, stopping at one of the doors at the end of the corridor. When it opened, she glanced down the stairs. "What's down there?"

"The basement," he said. "That's where you'll find Garrett."

"No, that's were we'll find him. Start walking," she said, shoving him with a push of the gun. He started

The Calling

toward the stairs, much to her surprise. She followed him awkwardly down the steps, trying to keep the gun on him. She realized halfway down that she wasn't holding him at gunpoint as much as he was letting her do it. If he wanted to, he could have taken the gun from her by now. She wondered why he hadn't.

When they reached the bottom of the landing, she was shocked by what she saw. The basement was immense, the walls made of gray and black stone, and from what she could see, it looked like a torture chamber. An assortment of chains hung from the walls and the few wooden tables scattered about the room held metal instruments she'd never seen before. The cement floor held stains she didn't even want to contemplate and several cages were in the far corner. "Where is he?" she asked.

"Ms. Ford," Malcolm said, "I hate to disappoint you, but I'm afraid I can't grant you your wish. At least not yet."

Rayna turned to face him and pushed the gun harder against the side of his head. "Then I'm afraid you'll need to grow a new skull." Before she could summon the courage to pull the trigger, Malcolm reached up and snatched the gun from her, his thick fingered grasp clasping her around the throat before he shoved her back against the wall. Her heart sank when she realized what a fool she was.

Malcolm's eyes shifted from cool brown to a sunburst of yellow and orange. The bones in his face shifted momentarily before he clenched his jaw and chased the wolf away. Taking a deep breath, he tossed the gun across the room and stared down at her. "I had hoped it would be easier than this, Ms. Ford," he said. "I've tried repeatedly to accommodate you to no avail. Every comfort at my disposal has been granted you yet you treat me with disdain and make me appear a fool in front of my friends. I've treated you with respect and all I've received for my trouble is your constant complaining."

Rayna swallowed and turned her head, trying to loosen his grip on her neck. His fingers eased their pressure and she was allowed enough air to speak. "Did you honestly think I would just stand still while you ruined my life, Malcolm?"

"Ruined your life?" He stared at her for long, silent moments before laughing. "I'm giving you a new life! I'm granting you the privilege of becoming something more powerful than you ever dreamed. Why can you not see what I'm offering you is a gift?"

"Because it's not!" Rayna reached up and grabbed his arm, trying to pull his hand away from her throat. "You aren't God, Malcolm. You can't decide what's best for me or anyone else for that matter."

"What I offer you is a chance at becoming something eternal. A being so superior humans will worship you."

"Worship me? They won't worship me, Malcolm, or you for that matter. They'll fear what you are. They'll kill you on sight."

"No, they won't. Once you show them what it is we can offer them, they'll line up to become one of us. Imagine a world where the night breeds have free reign. Where we're free to live amongst the humans without fear of persecution. A world where we're worshiped instead of feared."

The Calling

"Is that your ultimate plan?" she asked. "To set yourself up as the new messiah? Do you honestly believe people will envy you, and your power, and line up to become one of the freaks in your show?" His grasp on her throat tightened and Rayna tried to catch her breath. His face shifted again, the bones sliding under his flesh and her eyes drooped shut as stars danced behind her eyelids.

"I have worked for years to bring this change about, Ms. Ford, and I'll not let anything stop me. I will have this with or without your help. The breeds will emerge from the dark. We'll live amongst the humans and once that happens, the world will be ours. It would be in your best interest to be on our side. Those who oppose us..." He smiled and released his hold on her, running a finger down her throat and stopping at the top of her blouse. "Play nice Ms. Ford. If you want your pet wolf to survive the night, I suggest you do exactly as you're told. Now come, our guests have waited long enough and I suggest you not embarrass me again. I'll make sure you live to regret it if you do."

Garrett grunted when Caleb slammed him against the tree. His arms yanked back around the tree trunk before the chains were hooked together at his wrists, quite effectively securing him. He gritted his teeth and pulled on the chains to no avail. In this position, without the wolf, he'd never break them and Malcolm knew it. That was why they'd fitted him with the collar. Once he tried to shift, the collar would expand, exposing the studs that would, quite effectively, decapitate him.

Caleb walked back around the tree, a smile on his face. "Are you as excited about tonight as I am?" he asked, bouncing on the balls of his feet. He inhaled deeply, letting it out in a whoosh. "There's no full moon but the chance of a hunt is quite invigorating. I know your girl is going to run."

"I'll see that she doesn't," Garrett said.

Caleb's smile widened. "She's not as well trained as you are, Garrett. She'll run. Mark my words and when she does…" He laughed, cupping the bulge in the front of his pants before moving to the center of the clearing. "Do you think she'll scream for me?"

Garrett knew Caleb was baiting him and it was working. It took every ounce of control he had to keep the wolf at bay. He had no illusions as to what Caleb would do to Rayna given the chance. He'd claim her for no other reason than to prove he could. Caleb didn't want her. Not like he himself did. No, Caleb wanted to possess her, to claim her as his own and add her to his little pack of trophy wolves. To make her a plaything to his whims.

The wolf stretched under his skin and slid against his bones. The longer Garrett stared at Caleb, the more the wolf wanted out. It knew his mate was in danger and protecting her was all he was concerned about regardless of the fact they'd both die the minute he reached the surface. It was up to him, the man, to keep the beast contained. One tiny slip could end both their lives, and Rayna's.

The Calling

He glanced over at Bryce, watching him stare at Caleb and wondered exactly how tonight would play out. He'd had a very interesting conversation in the basement and hoped like hell he could trust the very few hands he'd placed Rayna's life in. If he'd misjudged them... He didn't want to think about it at the moment. He'd worry about that when the time came. For now, he had to stay clear-headed and not lose it. Easier said than done.

The ritual ground was crawling with people. If people was what you wanted to call them. Rayna saw the shifters from the dinner party, and Sabriel, the vampire, gathered around the large rock face. They were chatting amongst themselves, smiling and watching the growing crowd.

The atmosphere was jovial, everyone in a festive mood. She wished she could share in their joy. Knowing she was about to become a midnight snack for someone caused her stomach to cramp and her vision to blur. Malcolm led her to the center of the circle and stopped, his hold on her arm tightening to this side of pain. A glance around the clearing showed the eager faces of those who wanted to live amongst the humans. Faces of people who were here for no other reason than to watch her be attacked.

She turned her head to look over her shoulder and saw Judith. Their eyes met for a brief second before the woman looked to her right and back again. Rayna followed her gaze and saw Bryce. He was staring at her. His arms were folded over his chest and the piercing look in his eyes held her in place. She wasn't sure where his loyalty lay but he was the only person there who had showed her any compassion. When they were captured in the forest, he'd kept her safe from Caleb. She wondered if he'd help her now and was willing to beg him on one knee if she knew it would help.

He took a step to his left and that's when she saw Garrett. He was behind Bryce, his arms pulled tightly behind him and around the tree at his back. "Garrett!" She jerked away from Malcolm when Garrett looked up and she stumbled, hitting her knees hard before righting herself and running. Malcolm's shout for her to stop followed her across the clearing. She ran headlong into Garrett, stopping only when her body collided with his. "Are you all right?" she asked.

"I'm fine," he said, smiling. His smile vanished a second later. "What the hell happened to your face!"

Rayna reached up, fingering her cheek where Carmen had punched her. It was tender to the touch and she could only imagine what it looked like. "Carmen." His eyes changed colors in an instant. "I'm okay," she said. "It just hurts when I smile or talk." He stared at her, his gaze roaming her face and she saw his jaw clench when he looked at her neck.

"Did Carmen do that as well?"

Reaching for her neck, she felt the tenderness and knew it was probably pretty shades of black and blue. "No," she said. "Malcolm wasn't too fond of me shoving a gun into his face in front of all his friends." Garrett looked across the clearing, his deadly gaze on Malcolm.

"I'm going to get you out of this," he said. "Trust me."

"I do trust you."

He looked back at her. "Then promise me, no matter what happens, you won't run."

"I won't."

"I mean it, Rayna. Caleb wants you to and he'll hurt you if you do. Promise me you'll stay put. I won't let him hurt you."

"I promise."

The crunch of leaves and rock under someone's feet caught Rayna's attention and she turned her head, looking back over her shoulder. Malcolm was standing behind her, smiling. "If you're quite through, Ms. Ford, we do need to get started."

"Malcolm, I will rip your throat out if you so much as touch her," Garrett yelled.

"I don't plan on touching her, Garrett," Malcolm said, grinning. "Caleb will do that for me. You had your chance to do the honors. You refused, if I remember correctly."

Rayna was snatched back into place at Malcolm's side a moment later. "Now," Malcolm said. "I suggest you don't try anything heroic, Garrett. That pretty little collar you're wearing, I'm told, doesn't go with your fur coat." Malcolm reached up and patted Garrett on the neck, his fingernails elongated and clicked against the thick metal of the collar.

Garrett held Rayna's gaze as she was led back to the center of the clearing and she only looked away when Malcolm turned them and faced the rock ledge. "Now, do behave, Ms. Ford. I'd hate for you to embarrass me again. I can promise you you'll regret it this time."

Malcolm smiled and straightened his shoulders, pulling her closer to him. "My friends," he said. "I do apologize for the delay but let's not wait any longer, shall we? Ms. Ford has graciously consented to be our spokesperson in our transition."

Rayna tried to jerk her arm from his grasp and yelled when he wouldn't let go. "The only thing I'm going to do for you is have you arrested, Malcolm!"

"On what grounds?" he asked, looking down at her.

"Stalking. Kidnapping. Assault. Should I go on?"

"You'll do no such thing," he said, waving his arm in the air to dismiss her comment. "Caleb, whenever you're ready."

Malcolm released her arm, walking across the clearing to join the others at the rock face and for a brief second, she contemplated running. Garrett's words came back to her then. "Don't run," he'd said. "Caleb wants you to run." Clenching her jaw, and the desire to do exactly what Garret told her not to do, she locked her knees and tried to hold still.

Caleb advanced from the far side of the clearing. The smile on his face as he stared at her caused her stomach to cramp. The bastard was going to enjoy this. She could tell by the swagger in his walk, the slight tilt of his head. He was again dressed in nothing but his jeans. The moonlight glowing through the trees overhead shined down on his blue hair and pale skin and caused him to look down right ethereal. Her pulse started racing when she saw his eyes shift from cool blue to that eerie wolf orange.

When Caleb reached her, he grabbed both her arms and jerked her to him, his body flush with her own. She could tell how excited he was. Proof of it lay hard and solid against her stomach. She swallowed audibly and glanced around the clearing. Mitch was the first person she saw. He was trying to fade into the background as he eased his way to the tree line. His eyes were huge, horrified. Much like hers were, she imagined. Another glance around and she saw Carmen, blood still oozing from her cheek. For someone who'd had half their face ripped off, she was still able to pull off a very smug look. Bryce was still standing near Garrett and for the first time, she saw something on his face that shocked her. Sympathy and remorse. She grabbed onto it and begged for his help. "Bryce, don't let them do this!" He looked away, glancing at Malcolm. "Please!"

She looked to Garrett and barely got a glimpse of him when Caleb grabbed her chin and brought her attention back to him. He was smiling at her. "Once I turn you, I'm going to ride you until you beg me to fuck you just a little bit harder," he said, his face only inches from her own. "Since Garrett wasn't man enough to let that wolf out when he took you, I'll be sure you get to experience it."

He wiggled his tongue at her and leaned down. She wasn't sure if his intent was to kiss her or not but she wasn't taking any chances. She reached up and slapped his face. "I'd rather you kill me right where I stand than let you touch me, Caleb. Do your worst."

The rage that covered his face caused her body to tremble seconds before he squeezed her arms. He lifted his head and howled and every hair on Rayna's body stood on end as he did.

He shifted right in front of her. The clear liquid that always seemed to be present during a shift splattered her clothes. She turned away and screamed as his body convulsed, felt the bones in his hands move under his skin and heard the audible crack of shifting bone, flesh and muscle.

His wolf form was just as frightening as the others she had seen. He was on two legs, like Garrett's wolf always was, but the hair on his body was a pale auburn. The inside of his ears and the hair around his mouth was black. His lips pulled back for a moment and she saw teeth that made her knees go weak. Teeth she knew were going to be in her flesh any second now. He was going to bite her. Infect her and turn her into a werewolf. She would have laughed if she weren't scared shitless. She turned her head to look over her shoulder at Garrett as her vision blurred with tears. He was still chained to the tree but struggling.

A jerk of her arm and she screamed again, turning her face away from the horror in front of her and struggled in his grasp. His claws bit into her arms, his loud snarls and growls drowning out her cries and she vaguely heard the sound of multiple growls, howls, and roars.

Caleb grabbed her by the hair, holding her head back and she screamed as he opened his mouth, those sharp teeth gleaming and wet coming toward her. She kicked and fought, looking for any way out of his grasp when she remembered. Aiming between his legs, she planted the toe of her shoe into his balls. His outraged howl nearly deafened her, his grip on her tightening until she knew he'd drawn blood and without thinking, she kicked him again and again.

He tossed her across the clearing as if she were weightless, the impact with the hard ground knocking the air from her lungs and caused spots to flash behind her eyelids. The noise in the clearing grew, angry voices shouting, and struggling to open her eyes, she saw why.

Garrett had broken his chains.

Sixteen

Garrett slung his arm in a wide arc, the chain still attached to his right wrist slashing across the pack members nearest to him and effectively knocking them out of his way. He stretched his neck and looked toward the sky, the howl he let out echoing through the trees and caused goose bumps to pimple Rayna's skin in an instant. He lifted his hand and grabbed the collar around his neck. A hard yank and the metal slipped off, freeing him and the wolf.

"You said it would hold!" Malcolm yelled and Rayna looked to where he stood. He was in front of Carmen, his fists clenched into her hair.

"It should have!" she said. "He couldn't have broken it on his own."

A chorus of howls followed Garrett's and turning her head and looking out across the clearing, Rayna could see a few of the others pulling at their clothes. They were shifting.

Malcolm's guests sitting on the rock face were now on their feet. Some wore eager looks on their faces, others worried glances toward Garrett and those wolves now taking shape around the perimeter of the clearing.

A quick glance at Caleb showed him still bent over. Werewolves or not, their balls still hurt when

The Calling

kicked, apparently. Rayna struggled to her knees, wincing as her body protested. A sharp pain in her side took her breath and she grabbed her ribs, holding the spot right under her left breast. She knew she'd cracked something. After the way she'd hit the ground, it was a miracle she could move at all.

Malcolm moved back into the circle and looked wild-eyed at his pack. "Don't let him interfere," he said. "Restrain him!"

More of the wolves shifted then, doing Malcolm's bidding. The howls and throaty growls added to the chaos and as flesh melted into fur, claws and fangs poised to do battle, Rayna wondered if she'd come out of this alive.

Garrett shifted without effort and for the first time, Rayna watched without fear. She sat on her knees, watching the wolf take shape and knew in that instant, he'd do whatever it took to protect her.

She saw Caleb slowly straighten out of the corner of her eye and turned her head in his direction. His teeth were bared and she wondered then if instead of just infecting her, he'd kill her. Apparently Malcolm had the same thought. He stepped in front of him and yelled, "Only deep enough to infect her, Caleb!"

Malcolm was swatted away as if he were nothing. Caleb took a step toward her and she crawled to her feet. "Garrett!"

An ear-splitting roar and the clank of metal chains was all she got in return. He was fighting amongst the pack. A large circle of wolves surrounded him and she felt the helplessness of their situation in that moment. They were outnumbered.

Looking around the clearing, she noticed two things instantly. One, Malcolm was shifting. His wolf was pure gray. He was also on two legs and the look in his eyes was deadly. Thankfully, he wasn't looking at her. His gaze was fixed on Caleb. Two, Carmen was gone. She didn't know whether to be thankful for that or to be more scared. She knew the woman would kill her given the chance.

She didn't realize she was backing away until she came into contact with a tree. She yelped in surprise and knew it was a mistake the moment the shadows of the forest engulfed her. There was nowhere to go. The forest was at her back, a massive, pissed off werewolf at her front. If she ran, Caleb would be on her in an instant. Another glance at Garrett and she wanted to cry. He was surrounded.

A deep breath in to try and settle her nerves and she knew it was either stand there and get eaten, or run. She took her chances and ran for Garrett.

The rapid click of heavy footfalls followed her and she was afraid to look. She only made it half way across the clearing before a growl sounded behind her moments before she hit the ground. She screamed, tried to crawl away and was blinded by tears as she was grabbed by the ankle and roughly flipped over onto her back.

Caleb was leaning over her, his orange-yellow eyes blazing as his head lowered. She tried kicking him again, screamed into his face as he neared her and beat against his chest. The noise in the clearing grew, multiple shouts heard and as quickly as Caleb appeared, he was gone in a whoosh of fur, his startled yelps music to her ears.

The Calling

Rayna let out a choked sob as she watched him roll across the dirt floor of the clearing, tangled with Bryce who was still in human form.

They both snarled and she saw Bryce slowly start to shift. Caleb hit him and knocked him to the ground, not letting up as the wolf slowly emerged under him. When Bryce's wolf finally surfaced he rolled until he was able to crawl to his feet. Caleb followed him and wasted no time in attacking. The heavy pawed swings drew blood, teeth bit into flesh and Rayna scooted back across the ground and looked for Malcolm, her eyes widening when she saw him engaged in his own battle. Another wolf was fighting him. Malcolm batted him away effortlessly, drawing blood and a pained yelp. She winced as the wolf he was fighting was grabbed and jerked from the ground before Malcolm bit into the side of his neck. Another howl echoed off through the clearing as Malcolm tore a chunk of meat away and spat it on the ground. She turned away and willed herself not to vomit.

A look around the clearing and she saw wolf attacking wolf. Malcolm's plan was crumbling. The pack was divided, fighting amongst themselves.

Climbing to her feet, Rayna edged closer to the trees, trying to keep her eyes on Garrett, Malcolm and Caleb's fights and didn't know which way to turn. Every inch of the circle was covered with massive, snarling werewolves. She understood now how fighting determined who was strong enough to lead the pack. Anyone able to survive such a brutal assault deserved to be king and from where she was standing, there was only one wolf that deserved that title. There wasn't a doubt in her mind that Garrett would come out victor in this battle and a swell of pride bloomed in her chest as she watched him. He was fierce and never once relented. He tossed those attacking him away as if they weighed nothing and fought his way out of the tightly formed circle they held him in. When the last one gave way, he turned, his heavy gaze landing on her. She smiled at him, his head lowering a fraction in her direction before he turned and went after Caleb.

Caleb batted Bryce away and was advancing on him when Garrett reached him. He growled and turned, swinging his arm at Garrett and the heavy grunts and slashing clawed punches drew blood within moments. The air hung heavy with a coppery tang that coated Rayna's tongue with every breath. The entire clearing was covered with fighting werewolves and it was hard to tell who was fighting for whom.

A loud, shrill scream drew her attention back to Malcolm. He knocked his opponent away, sending the wolf crashing against the rock face and causing startled screams from those still watching from their safe perch. Confused voices shouted over the chaos and Rayna saw a few of the other shifters jumping from the rock face and run for the trees. Others preferred to join the fight, shifting into their animal form and jumping into the fray.

Malcolm turned and ran across the clearing toward Caleb and Garrett. The three tore at each other, their snarls and growls sending chills up her spine, and just as she was beginning to fear the unfair advantage Malcolm and Caleb had on Garrett, he lunged in a move so quick she nearly missed it, grabbing Caleb's head and twisting, the audible crack of breaking bone evident from across the circle.

The Calling

Caleb fell and didn't move.

She gasped, holding her breath as Garrett jumped for Malcolm, giving the packs leader a brutal slash of his claws. They cut across his chest, ripping through flesh, and blood splattered the ground as it ran down his body. They moved across the clearing, circling each other. They were both panting for breath, blood coated their bodies, and neither looked ready to give an inch. The fighting around the edges of the clearing slowed and Rayna saw every shifter present stop, their attention on the two in the middle. This is what they had all been waiting for.

She knew from what Garret had told her that taking on the pack leader was a significant thing. If he fought Malcolm and won, he'd earn the respect of the pack and in essence, become leader, but she knew that wasn't what he wanted. He didn't want to rule the pack.

Garrett turned his head, looking at those around him before facing Malcolm. "Don't make me kill you, Malcolm."

Malcolm snarled and straightened his spine. "It's the only way you'll get her off this mountain. I will have her, Garrett."

Garrett's shoulders fell a fraction of an inch before he shook his head. "No," he said. "You won't." He lunged for Malcolm, knocking him backwards and off his feet. The interest from the others grew anew as they tightened the circle around the fighting pair. Her view was blocked by the broad shoulders of the wolves in front of her but the sounds coming from the center of the circle were enough to cause the hair on the back of her neck to stand on end. Loud snarls and growls, a strangled yelp followed by a howl…

The circle broke apart abruptly and Garrett and Malcolm flew past the others in a blur of movement. They landed a few yards in front of her and for a brief second she couldn't tell who was who. The first one to their feet turned and leveled his gaze on her before running toward her. She screamed and stumbled back, trying to get away as he reached for her. It was Malcolm, his gray coat barely visible under the blood coating his body. She saw Garrett running toward him and she took a quick step to the left as Garrett swung at Malcolm.

Malcolm turned and grabbed Garrett with both hands, slinging him toward her. It felt like a truck hit her as his full weight fell on top of her and the pain was blinding. Her entire body ached and she gasped for breath. When Garrett rolled off of her, she saw Malcolm standing over them. His lips were turned back into what she assumed was a smile. Rayna jumped to her feet the instant Garrett swung at Malcolm.

He missed.

The feel of sharp claws ripping into her flesh caused spots to dance before her eyes. Fire raced through her limbs and she froze, staring wide-eyed at Garrett before looking down. The front of her shirt was shredded and she watched as blood bloomed brilliant red from the gash in her stomach.

Everything stopped. The growls, the fighting, her breath. She grabbed her stomach and looked up at Garrett, her vision dimming as she saw his lips curl back moments before he grabbed Malcolm and sank his teeth into his throat.

Malcolm's panicked screams echoed in her head as she hit the ground and she fought to keep her eyes open. She saw Garrett a moment later. Blood was splattered across his face, his breaths panted out unevenly as he leaned down and lifted her from the ground. She gasped as pain engulfed her limbs and Garrett's unearthly howl was the last thing she heard as she slipped into unconsciousness.

    The first thing Rayna noticed when she woke was the sun. It was shining in her face and she squinted and turned her head away. She could hear whispered voices and forced her eyes open, blinking against the light. Judith was at the door, talking to someone. She puzzled over her for long moments before turning to look around the room. It was the one she'd been given when she arrived at Malcolm's. Thinking of him caused everything to come back to her in flashes of images. The first shift she'd witnessed, being chased through the woods, seeing Garrett as a wolf and then learning he'd only alienated her to protect her. Their mad dash through the forest to escape Caleb and his men, their capture and the horrible fight she'd witnessed.
    She also remembered the pain.
    Looking down, she lifted the blankets, noticing she was naked under them. A bandage was around her stomach and spots of red dotted the white material. She dropped her head, and the blankets, and stared up at the ceiling.

Malcolm hadn't been the one to throw the killing blow, so to speak, but he accomplished his goal nonetheless.

Turning her head to the door, she licked her lips and said, "Judith."

The woman turned, her eyes widening before she quickly shut the door and walked across the room.

"Oh thank goodness," she said, sighing as she neared the bed. "I dreaded telling him you were still out when he came back up."

"Where is he?" she asked, knowing Garrett was whom she was talking about.

"I don't know," she said. "He comes in, checks on you, growls loud enough to put everyone on edge and stalks back out of the house. He's been gone for a few hours now."

"Is he all right?"

"He's not hurt, if that's what you're asking. Nothing life threatening, anyway. He had several nasty scratches but they had faded quite a bit last time he was up. He's more worried about you than anything." She looked away, fussing with the blankets and Rayna knew there was more.

She reached out, grabbing her hand. "What is it?" she asked.

Judith shook her head and smiled. "Nothing. There's no need for you to worry."

"Should I be worrying?" she asked.

"No, you shouldn't. Everything will be fine. It's just an adjustment for us all."

"What's an adjustment?"

The Calling

Judith walked to the foot of the bed and straightened the already pristine blankets. She glanced up quickly before walking to the windows and pulling the curtains closed. "With Malcolm gone no one knows what to expect."

Rayna stared at Judith's back, visions of the last time she saw Malcolm flashing in her mind's eye. His strangled screams could still be heard if she listened hard enough. "Garrett killed him, didn't he?"

Judith sighed and turned to face her. "Not everyone is handling it well," she said.

"Who?" The look on her face told her she was talking about Garrett. "Tell me, Judith."

She walked back to the bed and sat down on the edge. "Garrett's not physically hurt, so don't worry yourself." Rayna waited, staring at Judith until the woman sighed and hung her head.

"Judith. What aren't you telling me?"

"We all know it's because he's upset," she said, looking up. Her eyes were slightly wide and Rayna could see just a hint of fear hiding within their depths.

"What's because he's upset. You're not making any sense."

Judith glanced away, her shoulders dropping. "He hasn't been very pleasant to be around since that night." She adjusted the blankets again and looked at anything but her. "When Malcolm fell and Garrett picked you up, he carried you all the way from the forest back to the house without a word... We all thought you were dead. You were covered in blood. We didn't realize the majority of it wasn't yours until later but he, Garrett I mean, he was... I can't really describe it. I've seen Alpha's at their worst and we know to steer clear of them but we all knew he'd killed Malcolm. We saw it. Garrett was pack leader the moment Malcolm took his last breath and as wolves under his control, we're bound to him and him alone." She smiled sadly. "It hurts the pack when one of our own is wounded, whether that wound is physical or not, and Garrett was hurting. It took Bryce twenty minutes to talk him into letting you go long enough for us to tend to you. He was still angry and snapped at everyone and did nothing but pace around the room, growling. Half the pack is terrified of him now."

"Are they still afraid of him?"

"Most are," she said. "Like I said, he hasn't been here much and when he is, he rarely speaks to any of us. He just comes in, checks on you, barks out a few commands for your welfare and leaves again. We're not even sure where he's going."

Rayna touched her stomach through the blanket and winced before inhaling deeply. The pain lessoned a few moments later and she looked back at Judith. "It was bad, then? Where Garrett…"

Judith's face went pale and she looked down at the bed before nodding. "Bad enough," she said. She glanced up quickly before diverting her eyes.

Dread settled like a hard pit in her stomach, tear's burning the back of her eyes an instant later. "Am I infected?"

Judith sighed. "No one ever really knows at first," she said. "I think that's why Garrett has been so ill with everyone. He feels guilty and is lashing out at everyone and every thing because of it."

"So there's no way to tell?"

"Not yet. Not really. I mean, the fact you're still alive makes me thinks so," she said. "The gash was deep and you lost so much blood. There's no way a human could have survived that without a little help."

"Help?" Rayna said.

"The infection," Judith said. "I think that's what kept you from dying right off."

"So I am infected?"

Judith shrugged her shoulders. "The fact you survived the attack could be nothing more than you got lucky. Lycanthropy develops in stages. There's no test for it but a person knows when something is wrong inside their body. You'll know before the rest of us if Garrett infected you."

Infected. The word slammed through Rayna's head repeatedly like a drumbeat. All the running, the fear and pain, Garrett's adamant claims that he'd protect her came crashing down with the realization that one misplaced swing ended it all. Garrett had infected her.

Inhaling deeply, Rayna pushed the thought away and focused her attention back on Judith. "How?" she said. "How will I know if I'm infected?"

Judith smiled but it was only the corner of her mouth. It looked forced and when she again diverted her eyes, Rayna's chest ached as her heart clenched. "Well, your senses are usually the first change you notice," she said. "You're hearing will improve, your sense of smell, your vision. The brush of someone's hand against your skin can even feel different." She looked up and shrugged her shoulders. "It's not the same for everyone but it wasn't but a few weeks after my attack that I felt it."

"Felt what?" Rayna asked. "The difference in your senses?"

"No. I felt the wolf."

Rayna swallowed the sudden lump in her throat and stared up at the ceiling. The wolf. Did she have one now, waiting under her skin? Growing. The tears she been fighting came then and she turned her head away from Judith and tried to fight them. A gentle hand on her shoulder was all it took. The first sob took her moments before Judith wrapped her arms around her and tried to calm her.

Garrett walked into the house and didn't miss the startled yelps as he slammed the front door. The people on the bottom floor all lowered their heads and seeing them so submissive to him thrilled the wolf but made him, the man, sick to his stomach. They nearly pissed themselves every time he entered a room or looked at them. They hurried out of his way and fell over themselves to do his bidding the moment he asked for something. They were scared shitless of him and he didn't know why.

He started for the stairs and had climbed halfway up when he saw Bryce standing by the door of the sitting room. He stopped and walked back down, making his way across the foyer. "Let's talk," he said, motioning him inside and shutting the door behind them. When he turned, Bryce was standing next to the sofa, his head down. The bandage on his neck was still showing signs of

The Calling

blood but it was the first day he'd seen him when his color looked good. He'd been deathly pale for the past two days and regardless of how many times Judith had told him to lay down, the man had refused. Garrett sighed and crossed his arms over his chest and said, "Okay, explain it to me quick. I want to go see if Rayna is awake yet."

"Explain what?" Bryce asked.

"Why you unlocked that fucking collar and let the wolf out."

Bryce looked up and his shoulders relaxed. "I didn't like Malcolm's plan," he said, matter-of-factly. "I didn't like it when I was told, when I was forced to change so they could photograph me or when Malcolm arranged for Rayna to be here with the intention of infecting her. We had no choice but to do as Malcolm wished and I'm not the only one who disapproved of it. Most of the pack did. We weren't allowed to voice our opinion on the matter and were told if we mentioned it to Rayna, or her friend once they arrived, we wouldn't live to see the sunrise."

"Is that the only reason?"

The corner of his mouth twitched. "No. I knew if you were out you'd take care of all of them."

"You mean Malcolm and Caleb?"

"Yes." Bryce shifted on his feet and cleared his throat. "Things have changed since you've been gone, Garrett. Malcolm changed. His obsession with going public has been an ongoing issue for years. He ignored the pack and thought of nothing but himself. He talked about how great it would be to walk among the humans again but it was just talk at first. It wasn't until Carmen started crawling into his bed that she persuaded him to stop talking about it and just do it. He seriously started planning it after that."

Garrett walked across the room and sat on the arm of the chair. "So Carmen is who actually started all of this?"

"Yes. She's also the one who suggested Rayna."

He barely kept from growling. Why was he not surprised? "Have you seen her since that night?" he asked.

"No. No one has and I've had everyone looking for her. We haven't found Jacob or Stan either."

He did growl then. "Keep looking," he said, standing and crossing the room to the doors. "I want to know the minute any of them are spotted."

"Garrett? What are you going to do about the pack?"

"What am I going to do about them?" he asked. "What do you mean?"

Bryce shifted on his feet and glanced away. "You're pack leader now."

"No, I'm not," Garrett said, grabbing the doorknob.

"You killed Malcolm. That makes you leader whether you like it or not."

He stilled, staring down at the door before sighing. He knew this would be coming. Malcolm had even stated as much.

"With Caleb gone and his little rogue pack of wolves up at the mine, we need someone to stand up for us. Everyone is scared right now but they'll come around."

The Calling

Garrett turned then, his eyes narrowing. "Why is that?" he said. "What are they so damned scared of? They nearly piss themselves every time I walk into the room."

Bryce laughed but sobered quickly. "You do remember the night of the fight, right?"

He did. Well, most of it, anyway. "What does that have to do with anything?"

"I've been here for fifteen years and not once in all of Malcolm's tantrums did he ever scare the pack the way you did that night. We thought you were going to go berserk and kill us all."

"My girl had just been sliced nearly in half, by ME! How the hell should I have acted?"

"The way you did, I guess," Bryce said, shrugging his shoulder. "Still didn't keep any of us from fearing for our life. If anything, it only made it more plausible that you would."

He leaned back against the door, crossing his arms back over his chest. "So, they're just... waiting for me to go crazy and kill them all?"

"Yes."

"Then why haven't they run yet?"

Bryce grinned. "And go where?"

"Away from me?"

"Why would they leave the only pack leader they've known that could kick some ass without any help?"

"They're staying *because* they're afraid of me?"

"Basically, yes," Bryce said, grinning. "All any of us want is a place to belong, Garrett. A place we feel safe, with a leader who we all know will help us achieve that."

Garrett ran a hand over his face and shook his head. "I can't give them something I don't have in me, Bryce. I don't want this. I never did."

"It doesn't matter if you want it. It's yours regardless. Besides, if Rayna shifts, she'll need the help of the pack until she can control her wolf."

If Rayna shifts. The guilt returned then and cut through Garrett like blades of glass. It sucked the air from his lungs and caused his blood to run cold. He'd been terrified when he saw her cut open, blood spilling from her body faster than he could staunch it, knowing he had caused it. He had been the one to do exactly what he'd been fighting to prevent. He had infected her. Although it took weeks for a person to know if an infection occurred, he knew. It had. She wouldn't have survived an injury like the one he'd inflicted on her otherwise. The fact she was still alive told him she'd shift. All because he hadn't been smart enough. Hadn't fought hard enough. If he had never met her, she'd still be in Bluff's Point, driving the police department crazy as she tried to write her latest article. If he had never fallen in love with her, Carmen wouldn't have found her. Wouldn't have lured her down here. She wouldn't be lying upstairs infected by his hand.

Rayna was going to shift into a creature she feared and it was his fault.

"She needs you, Garrett. We all do."

He looked up then, staring at Bryce for long moments. Rayna didn't need him. He'd caused her enough problems already and the pack would only suffer in the long run. They didn't need him, regardless of what they thought. He turned and left the room without a

The Calling

word. He saw Judith hurrying down the stairs. One look at her smiling face and he knew. Rayna was awake. As much as he wanted to see her, to make sure she was all right, he couldn't. She was better off without him. Because of him, she was now a creature even he loathed.

Seventeen

Rayna stood on the ridge and stared out over the mountain. She'd spent every minute she could here, looking out at the vastness of the world and trying to find her place in it. Three weeks since Malcolm's death and she was finally healed. The fact the wound had healed so quickly told her all she needed to know. At some point, she was going to shift.

Judith told her it could take months for the wolf to grow strong enough to show herself but eventually, she would emerge. Her senses had improved, just as Judith said they would, and much to her surprise, she'd been pleased by it. She saw the world more clearly now and smelled mountain laurel from half a mile away. Her agility had improved and much to her amusement, she could transverse the forest almost as well as Bryce could.

She'd been infected and knew the wolf was coming but the one man she needed to help her through it all seemed to disappear as quickly as he came.

Garrett had avoided her like the plague since she woke up. She saw him everyday sneaking around the house but very rarely had she spoken to him. He'd dart away the minute she caught him watching her and she was frustrated as hell. After talking with Bryce she knew why. Garrett felt responsible. His guilt kept him away. After everything they'd been through, he was still hiding from her. Waiting in the dark, watching her.

She turned when she heard someone behind her and smiled at Judith as she topped the hill.

"Bryce said he was going to build you a bench to put up here," she said as she approached her. "Or we can just build you a cabin, if you prefer."

She grinned and looked back over the mountain. "It's quiet up here," she said. "It gives me time to think."

Judith stopped beside of her and sighed. "It is pretty here, isn't it?"

"Yes. You can see for miles in either direction."

"It's one of the reason's we settled here," Judith said. "Well, that and it's isolated. It serves its purpose, I suppose."

Rayna turned her head, looking over at her. "Judith, did you want Malcolm's plan to succeed?"

The woman blushed before staring down at her feet. "I didn't want you hurt, if that's what you're asking, but yes, it would be nice to get off this mountain eventually."

"Then why don't you?" she asked. "Garrett lived in the city for years and no one knew. Hell I spent six months with him, practically living with him or him me, and I never knew."

"Garrett is stronger than we are. He can control the wolf better than most."

"Then learn how to control it better."

Judith smiled and nodded. "I've been living here since Malcolm got us out of that facility, Rayna. I'm not sure I can function in the real world. I'm too scared to try." She glanced up at her before shrugging her shoulders. "I suppose if I really wanted to leave I could."

"You all could," Rayna said. "And you'd solve a lot of your problems, Garrett being one of them. He doesn't want to lead this pack. I think that's part of the reason he's been hiding."

"I know."

"Of course, he's hiding from me, too," Rayna said. "If I just knew where he was hiding I'd go drag him back by his cowardly tail."

Judith laughed and said, "He's at Jacob's cabin."

"I've checked there."

"Bryce said he's been holding up there and runs the minute he sees you coming."

"What!"

Judith nodded her head and grinned. "He's there now if you want to ambush him, but don't tell him I said so."

"Ambushing him is probably the only way I'm going to be able to talk to him."

"He'll come around."

"He hasn't so far."

Judith sighed and shook his head. "He's just being pig-headed. Wolves are like that, you know. He thinks he's doing what's best for you."

"No, he thinks he's responsible so his guilt keeps him away."

"That too," Judith grinned.

They were silent for long minutes, both lost in their own thoughts. Rayna wasn't sure what to do about anything anymore. She'd already called Clive and quit her job. Mitch had done the same. The entire office thought

The Calling

they'd eloped, according to Mitch, and she wouldn't put it past her friend to have let that piece of gossip slip out himself. He'd seemed genuinely happy since the Malcolm ordeal and whatever Carmen and Caleb did to him was finally being accepted now that they were gone. Of course, no one knew where Carmen was so the fear she would show up was still there. Jacob was still missing as well. All any of them could do now was wait. It was the waiting that was the hard part and not having Garrett there made it harder. She was scared and couldn't tell a damn soul. Scared of the changes in her body, scared of the upcoming shift, scared she'd lost Garrett. "What am I supposed to do," she asked, more to herself than to Judith.

"What do you want to do?"

She laughed and shook her head. "Beat the shit out of him for leaving me again when he promised me he wouldn't."

"I would pay to see that." Judith said, turning her head toward her.

"I just don't get it," she said, sighing. "Before we were caught he told me the wolf wanted to claim me. How could he say that then leave me? Are wolves that fickle?"

Judith laughed. "Oh no. If he said the wolf wanted you I can assure you him staying away is more painful for him than it is for you."

"Then why?"

"Because he's a man and we all know they think they're doing the right thing when they aren't."

"What am I supposed to do then? Wait him out?"

"Well, you can always force him to choose." Judith grinned at her and tilted his head to one side. "Exactly how bad do you want him?" she asked. "Because I know of a way to get his attention and I can promise you, he won't be the one running away."

Rayna didn't even pause as she reached the door of the cabin. She shoved it open without knocking, listening to it hit the wall as she looked around the room. She saw a stunned expression cross Garrett's face, his eyes widening as she marched across the room to the sofa where he sat before she planted one knee between his legs and grabbed his head with both hands, leaning down to kiss him. She forced her tongue into his mouth, taking what she wanted and didn't give him time to protest. She pressed her body against him, her fingers tightening in his hair until he tilted his head, deepening the kiss and moaned into her mouth. When he raised his hands and touched her, she jerked away from him and started backing toward the door. "I need a mate," she said. "And I choose you, Garrett Kincaid. If that wolf of yours wants me, then have him catch me."

She turned and ran back out the door, jumping from the porch, and she'd barely made it into the trees when she heard him. She smiled at the sound of his feet hitting the wooden porch and wondered how far she'd actually get before he caught her. The crashing of trampled brush she heard behind her told her not very far.

The trek through the forest was nothing to her now and she pumped her arms at her side, raising her legs

The Calling

high as she jumped fallen limbs and small bushes. She weaved through the pines, darting in one direction before turning toward another. Garrett followed her with every turn, the sound of him behind her, chasing her, almost as exciting as what she knew was coming.

When she heard the rushing water of the creek, she knew he was just prolonging the chase. He could have caught her minutes after they entered the woods and she grinned knowing he was enjoying their game as much as she did. The moment she saw the creek, she turned and ran for it, running across the shallow rock bed to the other side. He followed, the splashing from the creek as he ran across growing closer as she ran up the bank and back onto solid ground.

He caught her before she got her feet under her good.

They crashed to the ground, the air leaving her body in a whoosh as he landed on top of her, his hips pressing into her butt. He was already hard. He ground himself against her as his arms circled her waist. She squirmed and clawed at the ground, trying to free herself and let out a startled yelp as his blunt teeth bit into the side of her neck. He pushed his hips against her backside and reached under her, sliding his hand between her legs and cupping her through her jeans, squeezing. Sparks of need zapped through her limbs and she squirmed against his hand.

The hold he had on her neck slacked, his teeth coming away from her skin. "Lay still," he rasped in her ear. "Don't move."

She stilled under him, her heart slamming against her ribcage. She knew what he was doing the moment he laid his head against hers and wasn't having any part of it. It wasn't going to be that easy for him. She wouldn't play the submissive. If he wanted her, he'd have to fight her for it. She smiled to herself before bracing her arms and arching her back, trying to buck him off of her. He growled, his hold on her tightening as she clawed at the ground and tried to get away.

Kicking her feet she was able to dislodge him enough to flip over. He reached for her, pinning her to the ground with one arm across the front of her chest. She was panting for breath, struggling under him and raised her head, biting into his shoulder. He yelled and grabbed the back of her head, his fingers twisting in her hair before she released her hold. He grabbed her arms, jerking them over her head. The look on his face nearly made her come. He looked like he wanted to eat her alive and god help her, she nearly wanted him to.

"Rayna, I'm warning you." His eyes had bled to wolf amber, his voice raspy and thick, guttural. She bucked under him, kneeing him in the thigh before he growled and trapped her legs between his own. He lowered his head, his growl vibrating in her chest. "You don't know what you're doing."

"Yes, I do," she said. "I don't need a puppy for a mate, Garrett, I need a wolf. Either prove you're that wolf or I'll find another."

She knew her choice of words were wrong the second they were out of her mouth. His eyes blazed, his deep, rumbling growl sent chills racing up her spine before he took her mouth hard. He forced his tongue past her lips, pressing her head into the ground and she gave as much as she got. The moment he loosened his grip on her arms she reached up, wrapping her arms around his shoulders and held him to her. The rumbling in his chest grew louder, his hips pressing into her just a little bit harder.

Rayna sank her nails into his shoulders before raking them down his back. She grabbed the hem of his shirt, jerking it up so she could touch his bare skin. He lifted, helping her remove the shirt. She panted for breath as he nibbled on her lips, bit gently across her jaw to her throat. She barely contained the moan wanting to escape as he sucked at her flesh and tried to remember the things Judith had told her. She ticked them off inside her head and knew she'd only accomplished a few of them.

When Garrett's head lowered, his lips sliding softly across her skin to the top of her shirt and nuzzling his face into her cleavage, she bucked under him, grinning when he landed on his side. She flipped over, crawling to her knees, getting one foot on the ground before launching herself up. He grabbed her before she could stand completely, wrestling her back to the ground. He was on her back again, panting in her ear. "Rayna, don't make me hurt you."

She looked over her shoulder at him and reached up, grabbing a handful of his hair and pulled his head down to her. "And don't puss out on me. Where's that wolf that wanted me? If you're too afraid to take me, then maybe he will!"

He growled again and reached for the collar of her shirt. The material ripped as he jerked, baring her back to him. She'd gone without a bra and he took advantage of the fact, pulling her to her knees and cupping her breast in his hand, pinching her nipple to the point of pain. His free hand worked on the snap of her jeans. He latched onto her shoulder, his blunt teeth sinking into her skin deep enough for her to hold still or cause herself pain. He worked her pants and underwear down her thighs before he let go of her and pushed her head and shoulders to the ground. She heard the zipper on his pants moments before he spread her thighs as far as the jeans around her knees would let him. The velvety smoothness of his cock brushed against her folds, slipping against the wetness he found before he lined himself up and slammed into her with a triumphant growl. She gasped and clawed at the ground, her cheek pressed into the grass. He rode her hard, her breath forced from her lungs with each violent surge of his hips, his fingers digging into her flesh.

Rayna pushed back against him as his grunts filled the air. The sound of wet flesh meeting and the musky scent of sex caused her stomach to tighten, the tingles running laps through her limbs caused sparks to flash in tiny zaps along her veins. She clenched her body, squeezing him inside of her. She heard him say her name before his arms circled her chest, his hands grasping her around the front of her shoulders. His chest was flat against her back and he nuzzled her neck, his growls growing louder as he fucked her. "Do it, Garrett. Make me yours."

There was only a moment of panic as she heard shifting bones before sharp canines sank into her flesh. He shoved her to the ground, his weight holding her still as he drank her down, his hips pounding into her from behind. She screamed through the pain and convulsed around his cock, her entire body shuddering as she came. He slammed into her relentlessly before pushing once,

The Calling

twice... holding his hips tightly against her as he spilled himself inside of her then stilling.

They fell to their sides, him still buried between her legs. He removed his teeth from her neck, his lips and tongue lapping and soothing the torn flesh as his hands stroked her fevered flesh. A soft rumble emitted from his chest and vibrated against her back. She heard him whisper, "mine," against her neck and for the first time in her life, she felt like she belonged. She felt safe and protected and knew without a doubt, the man, the wolf, at her back would do anything to protect her.

Her throat tightened and she blinked back tears as her chest swelled with love for him. She grabbed his hand, lifting it to her mouth and kissed his palm. "I love you," she whispered.

He stilled behind her. He gave the bite mark a lazy swipe of his tongue, his lips caressing the torn flesh before he lifted his head. She held her breath, staring at the ground. When he leaned up and grabbed her chin, turning her head to him, the look on his face nearly did her in. "I've loved you from the moment I first saw you, Rayna. I wanted you the first time you smiled at me in that dingy little bar. Wanted to make you mine forever the first time I kissed you." He leaned down, his lips tasting and teasing her own. "I've always loved you... I adore you."

She couldn't hold back the tears at his soft admission and turned, wrapping her arms around his neck. After everything they'd been through, this moment made it all worth it. She'd do it all again ten times over if it brought them back here. Everything before this moment seemed trivial to her now. The horror's she'd seen and lived through, the realization that she was going to be a creature she had feared… it was all worth it. Garrett loved her and he was hers. Her mate.

Epilogue

Garrett watched everyone fill into the clearing and wondered for the tenth time that day what he was doing. A month ago he'd stood in the trees and watched these same people shift and terrify his mate with the intentions of infecting her. Now, he stood before them, pack leader, watching them stare at him as the dying sun slowly gave way to stars. He didn't know what they wanted from him. He had no clue how to lead them but their fear of him had waned a great deal.

He owed that to *her* though.

Looking across the clearing, he watched Rayna laugh at something Judith said. Her thick mane of hair shined against her white shirt and when she turned her head, he saw the scar on her neck. The scar he'd left the day he'd chased her through the woods and claimed her for his own. The sight of it caused the wolf to slide against his bones, restless energy coiling in his limbs. He inhaled deeply, scenting her on the breeze. His senses tingled with awareness, his body tightening with eager anticipation for his mate. He smiled and resisted the urge to go to her. Even though he'd spent every minute he could with her since that day in the forest, it never seemed like enough. Just the scent of her in a room, the sound of her laughter or an innocent glance in his direction, and he wanted her. Wanted to feel her naked flesh against his own, to have her breath wash across his skin. To feel her limbs tangled with his as he made love to her. Drown in kisses that made his soul sing.

"You do realize there are over forty people here other than her, right?"

Garrett tore his gaze from Rayna and looked at Mitch before smiling. "There are? I hadn't noticed."

Mitch laughed and sat down on the rock shelf beside of him, staring out across the clearing. He sighed deeply before glancing back over at him. "You know, I never thought my life would turn out like this."

"None of us do," Garrett said.

Mitch nodded. "How long does it take?"

"How long does what take?"

Mitch glanced at his feet again. "Getting used to the idea that you aren't the only thing inside your skin."

"Do you want the truth or the pretty lie that will make you feel better?"

"The truth."

Garrett smiled at him and said, "You never get used to it."

"That's what I was afraid of."

"It gets easier though," he said. "After a while, it just becomes a part of who you are. You're never quite alone after that first shift."

Mitch nodded his head and looked back across the clearing. "Bryce said I might shift tonight."

"It's possible. You're wolf seems a little eager to show himself."

"Will it make me appear weak to say I'm scared shitless?"

The Calling

Garrett grinned. "No. Being scared is what keeps us human."

"I'll take your word for it," Mitch said. He slapped his hands on his knees and took a deep breath before turning to look at him. "So, are you going to shift with the others and join in the hunt?"

"No. I don't want to leave Rayna alone until she's ready to shift."

"So I take it you're staying?"

Garrett shrugged his shoulder. "For a while, I suppose. We can't decide on anything until after Rayna shifts for the first time."

"Will she tonight, you think?"

Garrett looked back across the clearing at her. "No. She can feel the wolf but she can barely call her enough to get her eyes to change color. It'll be a few more weeks I think."

"Well, I feel kind of sorry for you when she does."

"And why is that?"

Mitch stood and stepped down off the rock. He turned to look at him and grinned. "Rayna already has you whipped. Just imagine what that wolf of hers is going to do to your sorry ass."

Garrett laughed as Mitch walked away and stood up when he saw Rayna walking toward him. He reached for her, helping her up onto the rock face and pulled her into his arms. "What do you say we just skip this whole thing and head for the creek?"

She wrapped her arms around his neck and leaned up, giving him a soft kiss. "I'd love to but they're all waiting for you to impart your wisdom on them."

He snorted a laugh. "They're going to be sorely disappointed."

"No they're not," she said. "You're going to be a great pack leader. They know it too. It's why they're all so happy now."

"They're happy because you've kept me so distracted. They haven't had time to still be scared of me."

She shook her head at him and tightened her arms. "Have you decided on a second?"

He nodded. "Yeah. I'm going to pick Bryce." Her eyes widened slightly and he smiled at her. "He's the best one for the job. He only aided Malcolm because he was forced to. Besides, if he hadn't opened that collar and freed the wolf..." He shrugged and looked away from her. A finger on his chin brought his attention back to her.

"If you get all moody about that again, you're going to be sorry."

"Really?" he said, grinning. "And how's that?"

"You really don't want to know." He kissed her quick and hard. "Are you going to shift?" she asked.

"No. Not until later. I don't want to leave you here alone while the hunt is on."

She raised an eyebrow and grinned. "Well, just because you don't shift doesn't mean you can't hunt."

"And what exactly will I be hunting?" he asked, his arms tightening around her. "Whitetail?"

She laughed and leaned in to him. "And what if one of the others see my whitetail flashing through the forest."

"I'll make sure they steer clear of the creek."

The Calling

"It's a date then," she said. She turned her head, looking over her shoulder and smiled when she noticed everyone watching them. "I think they're ready for you, pack leader."

He sighed and let go of her before walking to the edge of the rock face and jumping down. Unlike Malcolm, he didn't feel the need to be above them. He walked to the center of the clearing before starting to speak.

Rayna sat down on the shelf, watching him as he talked to the pack. His pack. Her life with Garrett wasn't anything like she imagined it would be but she didn't regret a day of it. She was still fearful of the future, and of shifting, but she knew as long as he was by her side, everything would be fine. She had a man who loved her, a wolf who would fight tooth and claw to protect her and a pack of wayward werewolves she could now call family.

She smiled when he motioned Bryce forward and the joy on his face when Garrett announced him as his second showed on everyone else's face as well. There was a new king on the throne and the pack couldn't be happier regardless of what Garrett thought. He may have been a great cop but this was what he was meant to do. Leading this pack of wolves was his true calling.

A calling she was glad to be a part of.

The End

Other Books by Lily Graison

The Gathering [A Night Breeds Novel]

THE CALLING changed Rayna Ford's life forever, now in THE GATHERING, she will find out what she's truly become.

Rayna Ford didn't believe in monsters, until she became one herself. As a newly turned werewolf awaiting her first shift, Rayna puts all her trust in Garrett Kincaid, the man who accidentally infected her and changed her life forever. But when old enemies resurface and take her from the one man who vowed to protect her, Rayna must face her fears alone.

The Collective, the Breed leaders of all the preternatural species, haven't abandoned the dream of announcing their presence to the world and they still want Rayna to be the one who integrates them into human society. Her only chance at survival is to reveal the secret the breed leaders want her to show the world, but in doing so, she may alienate the very creatures she wants to protect and endanger her own life in the process.

About the Author:

LILY GRAISON resides in North Carolina, a stones throw away from the Blue Ridge Mountains and a few hours from the Outer Banks. First published in 2005, her debut novel won a Reviewers Choice Award. Writing mainly in the contemporary romance genre, Lily also dabbles in erotica, paranormals and westerns. When not writing, Lily can be found at her sewing machine creating 1800's Period Dresses or curled up in a chair with a book in her hand.

Made in the USA
Charleston, SC
19 April 2015